The Year

The Year

TOMAS ESPEDAL

TRANSLATED BY JAMES ANDERSON

LONDON NEW YORK CALCUTTA

This volume contains quotations and fragments from the following works: Petrarch's *Canzoniere, De vita solitaria, Secretum meum*, St Augustine's *Confessions*, Rainer Maria Rilke's *The Notebook of Malte Laurids Brigge*, Lisa Robertson's *R's Boat*.

Seagull Books, 2021

Originally published in Norwegian as *Året* by Tomas Espedal

© Gyldendal Norsk Forlag AS, 2016

First published in English translation by Seagull Books, 2021

English translation © James Anderson, 2021

This translation has been published with the financial support of NORLA

ISBN 978 0 8574 2 850 9

British Library Cataloguing-in-Publication Data
A catalogue record for this book is available from the British Library

Typeset by Seagull Books, Calcutta, India
Printed and bound by Versa Press, East Peoria, Illinois, USA

SPRING AUTUMN

SPRING

I want to write a book about the seasons
spring autumn summer winter
those bright days in April and June
the darkness of August
describe the months the weeks the days
the hours of the day
and the changes that repeat the same thing
forever in a new way.
Right now the wind is blowing in the treetops
of the pine forest
and the trees are bending submissively towards the earth
before straightening once more
to meet new gusts of wind
as they've always done
but one of the trees cracks
a quick dry sound
like breath bursting out of a lung.
It's the sound of cessation
drowned out by the wind that blows
a new season I
want to describe each and every day
for a full year
but where and when does the year begin

in the kitchen or in the living room
in September or November?

Why not begin the year today
Sunday the sixth of April?
It has been said
it has been written
that the first human being
arrived in the world on the sixth of April.
It's not hard to imagine
the world already there
its rivers and seas
dry land and mountains
fields and trees
plants and animals
everything is there
and he
the first man
comes walking along the river.
Where has he come from?
We don't know
he doesn't know himself
perhaps he's searching for a place
for someone like himself
he follows the river and arrives at a clearing
an opening in the forest
where the river narrows and turns calm
in a small lake.
He wants to rest here
he lies down in a scoop in the sand

feels the warmth of the sand
and falls asleep.
How long has he slept?
When he awakes a creature is sitting
on the sand staring at him
it's not an animal
nothing he's ever seen before
and yet he recognizes the thing
the eyes the expression
it might be his own
it's as if he were looking at himself in water
but this is something different
the face is thinner
the mouth wider
the body rounder
the breast softer
the neck long
slender arms small hands
she bends forward
sniffs him
he feels no fear
only a potent new unease
his heart beats faster
and the blood suffuses his body
like heat
like joy
he laughs.
She lowers her mouth to his stomach
presses her lips to his skin
and cautiously sticks out her tongue

tentatively licking his skin
and he watches his member rise
for the first time.
She sits astride him
looks into his eyes
and from that moment
they are indissolubly
man and woman.

On Monday the sixth of April
in 1327
Francesco Petrarca sees
Laura
for the first time.
In what's known as the Laura note
which Petrarch made on a loose sheet
after Laura's death
he wrote: That Laura
so famed for her personal attributes
and so long exalted in my poems
I first set eyes on
in my early youth
it was in the year 1327 in the month of April
during matins in the church of holy Clare
at Avignon.
And in the same town
in that same month of April
on the same sixth day
at the same hour in the morning
but in the year 1348

the earth was deprived
of the light of her eyes.
So Laura lived
in Petrarch's memory
from the sixth of April
to the sixth of April
she died aged thirty-four.
When he saw her for the first time
she was thirteen
from that day on
he loved no one
but her.
Petrarch was twenty-three
and for the next thirty-one years
he would write his songs to her
and after Laura's death
to her memory
in the great work *Canzoniere*
which has been called
a long and incomparable dialogue on the nature of love.
The *Canzoniere* comprises 366 poems
one for each day of the year
from the sixth of April to the sixth of April.

Today
Sunday the sixth of April
I'm taking the train from Nice to Avignon
to walk the road to L'Isle-sur-la-Sorgue
continuing on foot towards Fontaine-de-Vaucluse
where Petrarch managed to build a house

he could retire to
and write.
I flew to Nice
got a cheap room
near the railway station.
The room resembled a prison cell
a greyish-blue little room with a bunk
that folded down from the wall
a washbasin a window
overlooking the backyard.
When you opened the window steam
and fat fumes from the hotel kitchen
entered the room
and after a few minutes the walls
were covered in small black flecks
they kept moving
sometimes they flew through the room
towards the naked light bulb above the washbasin
or they settled on the wrist or behind the ear
of the man attempting sleep.
The unmistakable sound of mosquitoes
I tried to kill as many as possible
swatting the wall with a folded newspaper
the black spots turned red
small blood-red smudges above the bed
it wasn't my blood
whoever the blood belonged to
man or woman
her blood would soon
be mingling with mine.

It was impossible to sleep
in the small room
I lay listening to the traffic
rumbling in the night
in the city
the sound of cars and motorbikes
voices and shouts
they fell silent with the light
with the morning
and that dead silence
was almost worse
in an enclosed room.
I must have dropped off for a few hours
because when I tried to get up
my hands and feet were red
with countless bites
they covered my entire body
so many swellings and bites
that I lay there
feeling feverish
and gradually fever did develop
I'd become ill.

I was ill
but I was supposed to be in Avignon
for the sixth of April
it had been fixed.
For over a year I'd read
the songs Petrarch had written to Laura
and now I wanted to see the place

where Petrarch saw Laura for the first time
and I wanted to visit the house he'd built
in the valley of Vaucluse:
About thirty miles from Avignon I found
a small secluded valley called Vaucluse
where the loveliest of all springs
the Sorgue
rises.
Entranced by the beauty of the place
I settled here
with my books.
In this house where Petrarch lived
alone with his dog
the poet wrote his book
about living a retired and solitary life
De vita solitaria:
As I approached my fortieth year
and was yet in possession of my youthful strength
and ardour
I turned my back so entirely on my natural inclinations
that I quenched even
the memory of them
and it was as if I had never
seen a woman.

If it was possible to live alone
it was possible to love just one woman
all one's life
even after she'd died
and if that was possible

it was possible to live without other women
without sexuality
it was possible to live celibate
and it's possible
today
to live what Petrarch wrote
almost seven hundred years ago.
Today
Sunday the sixth of April
2014 I
am ill
I'm tired and exhausted after a sleepless night
but manage to get out of bed before midday
leave the hotel soaked in sweat
and walk the three blocks in the cold light of day
through the streets to the railway station
where the train will take me to Avignon.

Sunday the sixth of April:
It's natural that Petrarch compares Laura
to the sun she's a calendar
which breaks down all time
so she can be here for ever
the Laura sun.
Ah it's shining that sun
through the carriage window I miss you more and more
with each day that passes
each month
each year
that passes.

The train runs it speeds past beaches
along the blue coast at TGV speed past
the azure towns of Cagnes Antibes Golfe-Juan
Cannes you can't see them
these towns that fly past.
We can see the sky and we can see the sea and the sun
which follows the train and beats in through the window
strikes my face which swells in a double fever
burning heat on my skin in the compartment: IS IT POSSIBLE
TO OPEN A WINDOW?
No
it's not not at this speed
not in this Icarus-train.
I'm on the point of burning up
unable to breathe losing consciousness
darkness isn't far away.
The fever has taken hold of my body
and everything inside wants to come out and here it comes:
I puke into a plastic bag and look at the sun
it dazzles my eyes and pricks out a negative image
behind my eyelids: It's your face.
Then I pass out. Everything goes black. It turns cold.
I come round on the floor in the gangway
someone has placed me here so lovely
so good to lie down
so good to have been absent
so good to lie perfectly still and be carried
at enormous speed through the countryside
towards your destination.
Avignon. Sunday the sixth of April I find a hotel

in the middle of town a bright single room with air-conditioning
switch the conditioning on draw the curtains
it's dark and cold in the room so soothing
and quiet just the hum of the fan the cool
fresh sound
almost like wind almost like rain almost like home
almost like you were here
a fever-fantasy daydream: You stand by the window
pull open the curtains and are pierced by light
almost disappear
as you turn towards me
and vanish.

All worldly pleasure is a fleeting dream
Petrarch wrote
in the first sonnet of *Canzoniere*
and that line is a truth
just like the sentence: The meaning of a word lies
in the use that's made of it.
Petrarch's line is as precise and true
as a scientific law
or a mathematical formula: You can't hang on
to the one you love.
All worldly pleasure is a fleeting dream
it's a poetic truth
and we can test it against the sum of our experience.
Love will not last
it can't last unfortunately
it won't last luckily
at the bottom of every sorrow there is a joy

at the bottom of every joy there is a sorrow.
It is life itself that finds its expression in Petrarch's
line it is objective and hard
unyielding to the vagaries of time
a shard of nature
buried in mankind
like a sentence.
It's Monday morning I've slept for eleven hours.
There's nothing better
for someone on their own
than sleeping.
You're never alone when you're asleep.
Sleep is a gift
like love like oblivion
the sleeper loves and sometimes
deep in sleep
he's lost love
and himself:
Gone is his name
gone is his address
gone are his money and possessions
gone are his boots and clothes
gone are the city and its din
gone are the hotel and the park
gone are pain and worry
gone are sickness and fever.
I wake up
and order breakfast in my room
a croissant
black coffee

a glass of orange juice.
A thin strip of light through the chink in the curtains smothered
sun the wan yellow spreads through the room like
gentle heat another day of sun I have breakfast and go
to bed.

On Tuesday I pack my sack
fill my bottles with water
leave the hotel and walk
through the town out of the town.
Buy a map at a filling station
walk along the road
towards L'Isle-sur-la-Sorgue the island in the river
am told that it's dangerous to walk on the side
of the road the cars go fast here
like deathtraps for tramps and animals:
Dead hares and foxes by the roadside squashed
frogs flattened birds injured hedgehogs
on the hard highway slaughtered strays
shredded cats killed
by workaday murderers behind steering wheels
and lorries they don't give a centimetre of ground here
on this narrow road I
walk on the grass between the carriageway and the cornfields
those spring-green fields with sunflowers
and poppies in a dense thicket of flowers
wild flowers by the edge of the road
small flowers yellow orange red
flowers to the left black silver-grey shiny
automobiles to the right a thin line

between life and death between asphalt and the hedges
trees streams and the clear river
that passes beneath the road bridge
there is a big difference between someone
in a car and someone in a house.
I pass the houses they stand there so quietly
these sand-coloured houses
that resemble the landscape they come from.
The houses the gardens the fields
where vegetables fruit and berries are grown
you see North Africans working
animals and Africans in the fields.
The men greet me as I walk past
it's an old greeting alien
as when you greet a friend
or an apparition from a familiar land
or another time I
can't stop thinking about how beautiful they are
the workers the Africans
as all poor people are beautiful
in my eyes I
see the way they crawl through the fields
like the animals sheep cow goat horse
they graze here where the road forms a bend
and I'm brought to a stop
by a dog a shepherd's dog.
The old man looks like a scarecrow
he walks behind a large flock of sheep
with a whistle in his mouth
a wide-brimmed hat homespun clothes

thick boots a hard unshaven face
he's got three large dogs for protection
against predators three smaller sheepdogs
which keep the flock together as it moves
they're so well controlled
that I stand there spellbound
by the beauty of this performance
which is primeval
spellbound and frightened because the large dogs
sense me as a threat
and drive me away I
must go back the way I've come
and now the sheep farmer and his dogs drive
the flock off the pasture across the road
towards the farm that sits on a knoll
by the river just south of L'Isle-sur-la-Sorgue.
I arrive in the evening hungry
thirsty tired in that good way
it's dark and the small village shines
a string of lights is suspended on wires
above the restaurants by the River Sorgue.
I find a table white tablecloth
white napkins in the semi-darkness
filled with voices running water
the river so clear and transparent
the headwaters of the spring at Vaucluse
and here by the riverside I order
veal and potatoes a bottle of wine.
I ask the waiter if there's a place
I can sleep

you can sleep here he says
in a room above the restaurant
this is a pension.
The foot-traveller feels a deep
contentment gratitude the plate
is taken away he drinks some wine
scribbles in his notebooks smokes
a cigarette and writes down the leg
I have completed.
The Petrarchan leg.
Wednesday the ninth of April: Wake to the sound of water the water
that has flowed through your dreams during the night
and made you younger older.
The first river flowed through you suddenly
and the dream recalled something you'd forgotten.
The young woman who's your mother is sitting on a rug
on the grass close to the pool which is a bathing spot
on the river
she pulls off her sweater pulls the sweater
over her head it gets caught up in her hair
and she struggles with the sweater yanks and tears at
the sweater that wants to choke her to wrap its arms around her
neck and cling on won't let go
and now she's fighting for her life until with strong tugs she
tears at the sweater until it unravels and falls apart
and you see her naked.
The river runs beneath the house where I've been sleeping
the river runs through a tunnel or culvert under the floor
of the little room with a window over the water
the river it's like sleeping in a boat the bed floats

away in a darkness lit up
by dreams
about places.
Places you've been to and places you've never seen
now you're old in a strange place
which is here: You're sitting hunched forward in a wheelchair
at the restaurant by the river and you're eating with a woman.
Who is she? She's about to say her name
but you wake up with a start sit up in bed
and shout NO.
You wake to the sound of water the water
that flows beneath the house you're spending
a night in.
Today you're going to walk to Vaucluse and the spring the place
where Petrarch built his house on a little plot
where the river forks and tumbles down fast-flowing falls
past the house as if the poet lived in the river
which flowed through his house and what he wrote: One must extol
the countryside around this place for it was here she came into
the world beautiful woman.
It isn't hard to imagine
how Petrarch came riding from Avignon
on a narrow cart track by the river
it's the same landscape today
if we ignore the highway and the houses along the road
if we lift our eyes to the valley sides and the mountains.
Two horses two donkeys a load of books
his collection the books Petrarch called his daughters
two men brothers Francesco and Gherado riding
along the river about a day's journey on horseback

two donkeys ambling slowly on the muddy road
which follows the river and snaking climbs gently
towards the mountains that rise first as hills
the landscape rising and falling in rolling green
almost soft until the hilltops seem to rear
up in sharper edges and meet a mountain chain
mountains of seven hundred to a thousand feet that surround
and enclose the little village by the River Sorgue
not far from the spring in Vaucluse.
Petrarch described himself: not especially handsome
a round face large nose thin lips a hard
mouth and prominent eyes but with a mane of golden hair
and a powerful body strong he sits straight-backed on his horse
proud he's a writer poet well-read historian philosopher
friend of kings and pope prominent men letter-writer
politician Italian friend of Boccaccio admirer
of Virgil book-collector in love with Laura.
Now he's tired of Avignon weary of city life
he's searching for something else what is it he's looking for he's
got an idea about isolation and loneliness
about living a quiet and secluded life
in Vaucluse.
Petrarch wants to live a simple life
read write
that's what he wants.
He wants to organize his life around
reading and writing
he wants to write something important something big
something lasting that will outlive him
just as the *Aeneid* outlived Virgil

and to do something similar
well to be able to do the impossible
he must leave the city and its distractions
he must retire
he must isolate himself
he must build a solitude
in Vaucluse.
Francesco Petrarca rides out of Avignon
with his brother Gherardo
leaves Laura
so that he can write about her I walk
along the highway a stone's throw from the river the verge
a thin line between past and present
between life and death
between the silence of the mountains and the roar of traffic
just a small step to the right
and you're as dead as a flattened animal
on the road.
It was what I wanted once it isn't
long ago that I wished to die but now I want to live
that's all I want and I keep to the left
on the verge avoiding the cars and walking this Petrarch
leg so that I can write a book about love.
That's what I want to do.

Petrarch's house lies hidden behind a wall
a path passes through an opening in the wall
and ends in an open space
a sort of meadow where the river divides
flowing in several channels past the house and garden

which sometimes got flooded with river water
before Petrarch built a dyke a protection
for the flowers he grew roses lilies violets
the vegetable beds vines olive trees
he harvested in a labour that gradually became as
important to him as reading:
A life without books is a barren life
he wrote
and in his letters he describes his work in the garden
his walks in the mountains
the hunting and fishing
the nocturnal wanderings by the river:
Those who live busy lives don't live at all
he wrote
in the house
in the silence
in Vaucluse.
Just across the road from Petrarch's house
is a hotel
a large white timber building by the river's edge
dilapidated but with a residual splendour
which still emanates from the house and the few lamps
burning on the ground floor.
A couple live here
with their daughter in a flat
surrounded by all the empty rooms.
A narrow carpeted entrance hall with antique furniture
the furniture smells of damp of dust a faint smell of river
on the broad staircase to the rooms on the first floor

a cramped corridor doors the door opening on to the innermost
uppermost room which is a little attic
with a bed and writing table
a small staircase to the bathroom and a kitchen
table with a view of the river
this is where I put up
on Thursday the tenth of April
as the only guest
in the hotel.

Ah it's good to be alone
in a hotel
it's a sombre pleasure
to live within this great silence
in a small room.
After all you're here to feel the loneliness the lack
of the one you love.
When something hurts
you shouldn't avoid it
no
you should meet the worst
with all your weakness
and allow yourself to be destroyed.
You should seek out loneliness
to feel that you are alone
to feel that you are desolate
to feel that you have loved
to feel the love
that can obliterate you entirely.

Love
what do you know of it
until you've lost the one you love
until you realize you can't live without her
and yet you must live
without her.
Even though you think you'll die
without her
you'll live
and now you know what love is
and what it can do to you
here you are on life's border
with death
now you can choose
if you want to live or die.
And if you want to live
how you'll live without the one you love
how to live alone
without love
I don't know how.
The hotel is suffused with water
every night
the river flows from the river
filling the room with dreams
of friends who are no longer friends
people who are no longer people
whom water has turned
into water rats
water dogs
water men

with water faces
the face that will replace mine
and become my love's new lover
his face isn't strange
it belongs to a friend.

It's Friday Saturday I want to remain
here as long as possible
read and write
that's what I want.

Palm Sunday: There's always something about writing
on evocative days holidays.
Writing on Easter Saturday Christmas Day New Year's Eve
gives the words a special significance a special gravity
which is good for the writing hard on the writer
a special lonesomeness for the one writing
on high days
a special silence for the one sitting
alone
on New Year's Eve
writing.
I write on your birthday and on mine.
I write on all the difficult days
the day we met
the day we parted.
All those painful good days
which have got harder
almost unbearable now
because we're not together

because the days that were our days
have separated
into your days and mine.
What do you do with your days
which are our days?
Are things better for you now
without me
are you with someone else now
on our days
which are yours.
I try to love your days.
I try to love you more
than my days and your days.
I try to love your freedom
your life
without me
but I can't do it.
I want to
but I can't manage.
I can't love you
with someone else
I can't love
the other
him
and perhaps my love is
too small
and perhaps my love ought
to end here
but it doesn't

no
it turns into its opposite
and becomes hate
the hate of the other
of him
who is to be with you
and when he is with you
the hate of him
becomes hate of you I want to hate you.
I want to hate you despise you blame you
that's also a part of my love
the hate   the jealousy   my malice.
Janne light golden hair corn-gold long
long streaks of red and brown and some hairs
paler almost white
a hard tint of silver
in her hair
a coldness that has lodged in her hair
or a slight silvered bitterness
dry
something unfulfilled
an unexplored opportunity
just a silver tangle
in her hair.
That long hair
such a dominant part of her
that you hardly see her face I
never noticed her face
or even her body

until one day she put her hair up
with hairpins: That was the day I fell in love
with her.

For nearly two months we met each other
several times a week
and I never thought of her body at all
I walked beside that hair
that long unruly hair
which became a face
after a few days.
Mouth first
full lips
dry lips chapped (as it was winter).
I didn't think of kissing her
presumably because—for the first few months—
so many strange things came out of her
mouth she kept saying the oddest things
and I was completely occupied in listening
to her:
She made me laugh
I don't think I've ever laughed so much with anyone
as I did with her.
She spoke about herself
and now her face became clearer
it materialized around her mouth she narrated
her face into place
and now I saw how unusual her face was
old and young
those heavy shell-like eyelids

like in some fourteenth-century
lithograph
narrow arched eyebrows
above heavy eyelids
above half-open eyes
as if she was never fully awake
as if there was sand in her eyes
until the face suddenly broke out into laughter
and the eyes awoke.

Several times a week for almost two months
we went on long walks she
always clad in thick layers of clothing
heavy jackets knitted sweaters woolly hats mittens scarves I
never thought about her body for a moment
perhaps because it was so covered up
perhaps because she spoke so seriously so comically
that I had more than enough to do listening
as if for the first time I'd met a totally
unfamiliar person.
I was and remained infatuated
with her voice.
Her voice was red deep red it was
warm darkness
disturbingly deep
where did it come from
that voice she talked like an old lady
or a grown man.
She could say the most superficial the most foolish things
in a deep serious voice

and then I'd start laughing I'd never heard
a more beautiful voice.
We often walked to the cemetery at Møllendal strolling
along the path between the graves talking: for a long time
her voice hid her mouth
her face and her body I didn't see her
not properly
the way you always undress a girl
in your mind
when you're in love.

One February day it was snowing in the city new snow on our path
by the lake a thin layer of ice on Store Lungegårdsvann
birds on the ice the trees white
it reminded you of home
you said
we walked close together
you were wearing a long winter coat
fur hat mittens scarf and thick boots
as if we were off on some expedition: We
followed our usual route
but that day you wanted to come home with me
you'd never done that before
perhaps you wanted to see how I lived
perhaps you'd come to a decision at last
because when we got to my place
just after we'd come through the door
and you said what a lovely flat it was
old furniture leather sofa rugs
bookshelves

beautiful lamps
you took your clothes off
coat
sweater
blouse
pulled off your trousers
tights
pants
forgot your socks and unfastened your bra I
was flabbergasted totally flabbergasted
by this sudden nakedness
by this intense nakedness of yours.
Your breasts
your pale skin
your round bottom
thighs stomach back throat hands hair
sex
all this at once
so surprisingly sudden
naked
you stood naked in the living room
and I was in shock
I'd never been able to imagine a nakedness
so lovely a body so perfect as yours.
You kissed undressed me clumsily rough
as if you'd never undressed anyone before
tore off my clothes pushed me into the bedroom
it was practically a fight
as if you'd never loved anyone before
shoved and threw me down on to the bed

pulled off my trousers
held my penis hard in your hand
as if you'd never had a penis in your hand before
tasted it with your mouth sucked
as if you'd never had a penis in your mouth before
settled heavily on my penis and pressed yourself down
on it and gave a small cry
as if you'd never had a man inside you before I
lay beneath you
looked into your face
saw your open mouth
saw how you made love for the first time.
We didn't make love we wrestled
in bed and when at last we rested
I saw there was blood on the sheet
red
like your voice.

Maybe it's the heat which makes me think
of the cold   April which makes me think
of   February   it's hot
on Thursday the seventeenth of April in Vaucluse.
I wake early the sun is shining in through the window of
my hotel room daffodils in a vase at my bedside
writing materials on the table a rattan
chair a wardrobe with a mirror and the reflected image
of my coat on a peg behind the door
as if there were two of us staying in the room   but
there isn't only I live here I
and the want   of you.

I see Laura for the first time on Good Friday in Vaucluse.
A lithograph artist unknown nineteenth-century
copperplate engraving of Lauretta or Laura de Sade her picture
hangs in Petrarch's house in the library there
are several pictures of Laura in the house but it's
the portrait with the pearl necklace
which attracts my attention most: Your long golden hair
forms a plaited wreath around your face with its
narrow arched eyebrows above shell-like eyelids
half-open eyes terse mouth long neck and those
rounded shoulders that vanish into a thickly woven
cotton gown with no neckline a pattern of
right angles over the breast and around the neck
the pearl necklace I bought you in
Dubrovnik.

The loneliness of Easter Saturday is redoubled
by the day itself: One
who is all
is missing.

Easter morning casts out sorrow must be
the loveliest line I know
even though it isn't true
Saturday Sunday at seven past four
it isn't true
to wake
at this silent hour
which is neither morning nor night
which is a dead point in the day

when so many people kill themselves
just before life begins
is like waking in a great nothingness
a dark nothingness
a hole in life
that you've fallen into
during the night
and out of which no morning can drag you
because the morning is so far away
and because you've lost your faith
in all mornings
in all beginnings
the only thing you believe in
at that hour in the middle of nothing
is a welcome end.

Falling asleep sleeping sleep
helps
removes you from one place
deposits you in another
closer to day
where the beginning is possible
the beginning of the day: The light comes
you get up
get dressed
wash your face in cold water
open a bottle of wine
eat white bread
drink eat
switch on the radio

and feel your spirits rise: Today
you'll do something completely new
you'll drink the whole day
away.

On Sunday I leave the hotel walk
past Petrarch's house across the bridge
to the middle of town round a bend
following the river on the narrow street which is the way
to the spring at Vaucluse
past the restaurants souvenir shops stalls
selling pancakes burnt almonds candyfloss
among the crowds of visitors on outings
to the spring
which lies at the head of the valley
at the foot of the mountain
where the water wells up from the earth
clear and pure
in an eye
that overflows
not unlike weeping.
Not unlike tears
from the earth's core
from any ordinary eye
the water which collects in a river the River Sorgue
flows down the valley
as it did when Petrarch walked alone along the river
to hear the river nymphs sing
a song that no longer exists
or is it simply drowned out by the music

from the roundabout where the children ride round and round
on Easter Sunday
to the unheard song
of the river
flowing past. I walk by Petrarch's side
he's dressed in his Sunday best
like me
we are exactly the same age
we have the same interests
the same inclinations
he and I
we've got a lot to talk about.

One day when Petrarch was walking by the river
he heard women's voices
from the bank.
Carefully he walked down crept through the undergrowth
clambered over the boulders
towards an opening in the river a pool
where three women were undressing
to bathe.
He recognized Laura immediately
shut his eyes
he didn't want to see her naked.

Being dressed is always more beautiful
than nakedness
I say.
Not always he says.
She was much lovelier than I'd ever

have imagined and I'd always thought
of her with clothes on
never without
it never entered my head
and when I saw her naked
my love changed into something else
more serious deeper
something that kept me awake at night.

Formerly I'd loved her
now I wanted to possess her
own her
I wanted her to be mine
just mine
and that was worse
because I know
that love is bigger
than me
and my desire to own her for ever.
Love's beginning can also be
love's end
I knew that
when I saw her in the river
naked
for the first time.

We're at a restaurant by the river
a table on the edge of the terrace
beneath the coloured bulbs blue red
lights which mix with the light

of the full moon the starry sky the reflection
from the river we're having grilled trout
drinking rosé
being served by a young girl
who cadges cigarettes I like her at once
she talks to me as if I'm alone.
Will you have something with your coffee
she asks.
We'll certainly try some of the local Calvados
I say
two glasses please.
I don't drink spirits
Francesco says
he's been watering down his rosé
he's careful with alcohol.
In the book I've written: *Secretum*
I have a conversation
over three days
with St Augustine.
We discuss money
and vanity
and inner conflict
and being unhappy
and the search for a good life
we talk about love
just as you and I are talking now
says Francesco you look in good shape
with enough money it seems you're well-travelled travel
read you've written books and you're an acclaimed author
you say so why aren't you happy?

I've travelled so that I can read
Canzoniere here where the songs to Laura were written
in Avignon and this valley of the Vaucluse the house the
mountains
and not least the river
which is so present in the poems:
I want to read them carefully
almost like a meditation
perhaps as a solace
or an investigation:
Is it really possible to love the same woman
all your life
even if she doesn't return the love
and what sort of love is that
is it a greater love
or a self-deception
from which the writer spins sufferings
so that the songs have nothing to do with Laura
with love
but with writing
with finding the very source of the poetry
and thus the loss
of love.

You're being banal
Francesco says
leaning across the table
almost whispering
as if he's about to impart a secret
the secret is:

Even the loss of love
is love
he says.
And you are alone with this love
that's what loneliness is
he says.
To love and not to be loved in return
that's what a broken heart is
and because a broken heart can destroy you
it's one of the most valuable things you possess
you can use it to alter yourself entirely
a new life
he says
a poet must endure anything
if not he's no poet.

I light a cigarette
make notes in my notebook
the waitress comes and asks for a cigarette
can I smoke it with you all the customers have gone
you're the only one left do you want more to drink
before we close we'll turn off the lights but you can sit
here in the dark and write it's lovely there's a
full moon she says.
You haven't answered my question
Francesco says.
I'm unhappy
I say
because I was deserted
by the woman I was with

that was four years ago
and it still hurts
I don't understand why it doesn't pass
and sometimes I think it'll go on
for the rest of my life
that it will never get better.
Augustine quotes Naso: Old love
ends
when new love begins.
I don't want a new love
and I can't let go of the old one
even if I wanted to
it clings to inhabits
the whole of my being
deeply
as if this love
was me
is me
and the thought that my love for her
will be replaced by a new love
like replacing a pair of shoes
with a new pair
is an impossible thought.
New love
doesn't come
to one who loves.

The question when
you've really been in love is: How long
does it take for love to fade?

When she went
I was prostrated
ill
sleepless close to
breaking down later
I slept
a long sleep I did nothing
but sleep
slept away the days
drank away the nights
for a year it was: sleep away drink away the days.

That year was a dark year
almost black.

That year was almost
totally
lost.

I was totally black
almost lost
that year.

It's what Augustine called acedia
or aegritudo
says Francesco
on the terrace in the dark.
Augustine recognized the sickness in me
and charged me with it
told me to think of those in trouble
those who suffer poverty

those who are the victims of war
those who are fleeing
those who've been struck by disasters
told me to remember earthquakes floods
epidemics starvation
and to remember that I was secure and prosperous
whenever I hear about those whose sufferings
are greater than mine.

Augustine
says Francesco
said that the man who is secure
should be grateful
because the life he's been given
is a gift
you must learn to receive: Move out of the city
into the country and live a simple life closer to
nature rejoice in the seasons
and the changes around you.
Each day
each and every day
is a change
and we must learn to see
the day
as it is
a new day
different to the day before.

Friday the twenty-fifth of April: take the bus from Vaucluse
to Carpentras
sit in the square of the little town

eating an omelette
drinking coffee.
It's always nice to sit in a corner
watching the town and its life from a special vantage point
a point in the middle of town
and yet outside the town
the way the traveller is always outside what he sees
outside the place he finds himself in.
I'll walk the road to Bédoin
and on from Bédoin to La Colombe
where I'll have to stay the night
before I do as Petrarch did
climb Mont Ventoux
for no other reason
than to walk in the footsteps of the poet
who was the first to describe
the ascent of a mountain.
Petrarch did it on the twenty-sixth of April 1336
with his brother Gherardo.
In a letter he writes
that he's suffering bouts of depression
looks out of his window towards Mont Ventoux
and decides to climb the mountain.
The letter in which he describes the climb
is a masterly piece of prose.
Petrarch sums up the past ten years
and thinks about what is to come
his move from Avignon
his retreat to Vaucluse
the books he's going to write there

simultaneously he describes walking
so that the ramble becomes a fusion
of reflections and descriptions of nature
an essay
about climbing a mountain.
And when he and his brother reach the summit
that windswept height
Mont Ventoux
where he enjoys the view
the joy of being able to see so far
Petrarch feels the need to dip into
Augustine's *Confessions*
which he always carries with him.
He opens the book at random
and reads to his brother: Men walk
to admire the high mountains and the great rivers
and the movements of the stars but forget to examine
themselves.
I
leave the town
it's always nice to walk
out of a town to walk through the outskirts
their shopping centres parking lots filling stations
and suddenly feel the change from town to country
a new smell a silence a new alertness
as if you see everything with completely new eyes
and see it all for the first time a flock of birds
flying up the wind moving the trees the light on the
flowing river all the simple everyday things
that repeat themselves

so often that it's difficult to spot them.
A slight warmth rises from the moist path
a mild warmth from the grass the flowers that grow
clustered together yellow by yellow red by green green by
yellow
on both sides of the path the good warmth
of spring a new spring bursting out
as I walk along the river
and feel the spring the warmth in my body swinging
my arms and singing too.
Rest eat
a meal of white bread butter sausage
water and wine.
Lie in the grass smoke a cigarette watch the sun
setting fire to the treetops the clouds are pink
with afternoon.
I walk into La Colombe in the evening
a small village of sand-coloured houses
on either side of the narrow road that curves
up climbing towards the mountains it's colder
here like walking from spring to winter
in the course of a single day it is Friday dark
moonlit tomorrow Saturday the twenty-sixth
of April I shall climb Mont Ventoux.

Wake up early
in the little room in the pension
eat a large breakfast in the breakfast room
of ham and eggs cheese and fruit coffee and juice.
Make a packed lunch buy bottles of water

a bottle of wine
pack my sack and set out
for the mountain.

The sun is shining.
All is well.
I miss Janne.

The mountain glows
its green foot silvery-grey sides the white
blunt peak Petrarch and his brother spent
almost twenty-four hours getting to and coming down from.
I must do it in half the time
to get back to the pension before it's
dark walk quickly along the road find the narrow
path that's supposed to lead to the chapel on the summit
the path is marked there's no chance of getting
lost as Petrarch did he wrote
that several times he found himself descending and
that it's not possible to scale a mountain
by going down first I climb through the forest
it's always the gentlest part
of a mountain trek walking through trees
broad-leaved trees pines the lovely smell of forest
the moist carpet of pine needles and earth
the shade of the leaf canopy it's like walking
through a tunnel under the light
the sunlight is fragmented by the treetops strikes
the ground in shafts and pools of light they move in the wind
dance on the path a silent music of light

in the forest I walk more slowly trying now to find
a rhythm which isn't too hasty
for the wilds: Weren't you going to think
some important thoughts like Petrarch did
on his mountain walk?

What have you done what do you want
for this
coming year?

The past ten years
have been another's life
in another life.
We live several lives
and there is only a slight connection
between you as a child
and you as a youth
and you growing up
and you becoming a father
and you losing your mother
and you being deserted by your children
and you becoming middle-aged
and you who will become old
and you who will die
and feel the proximity of death
more strongly than childhood
which you cannot properly recall.
It's almost impossible to link the fifty-three-
year-old man
to his youth and his childhood is long gone

even his adulthood seems remote
sometimes it can be hard to remember who
you were last year perhaps because you exist so vividly
in change
that it's change
that is life itself and sometimes
you can say
that the person you were yesterday
is no longer you today
yesterday you were married
today you aren't.
Then maybe it
happens one day
that you meet your great love
the one that will last the rest of your life.
But even love is in flux
one day loss
one day joy
one day jealousy
one day fury
one day rest
one day anxiety
one day heaven
one day hell
one day she's gone.
One day despair
one day hope
one day sympathy
one day desperation
one day sorrow

one day death
one day loneliness like you've never felt loneliness before
one day hopelessness
one day utter darkness
one day night
one day hate
one day she's lost for ever.
But love doesn't die
it continues
now you love someone who's gone
and who you'll never get back.
How is it possible
that your love goes on
year after year
even after she's wounded you
humiliated you utterly.
How can it be that you still love
her
are you ill
have you gone mad
yes no you feel as if you're normal
you also love
what's painful.
Perhaps she writes let me go
you must let me go now let me go
and you really want to let her go
you have let her go
but you love her
even after she's free.
Let her go

find a new love
or learn to be alone
to be solitary
with this love
which can't be supplanted
by anyone.

What will you do
in the
coming year?
This is what I think about
as I quit the forest
leave behind the pleasant shade of the trees
which are thinning and getting smaller an undergrowth dense
and prickly on the ground wild rose heather
and thistles that rip at the trousers
scratch the skin a good pain the sun
scorches the mountain opens
turns harder more exposed to light to wind
to the sun which has reached its highest point
in the sky the crystal-clear blue
interrupted by clouds
a cold wind that makes the sweat congeal
on my body I'm cold
in the heat.
What will you do
in the
coming year?
I think about this
as I reach the summit of Mont Ventoux

sit down out of the wind
in the small stone chapel
a dark cold room
in all that brightness all that expanse
on the windswept mountain top.
I've got no books in my sack
no Augustine no Petrarch
but get out the packed food I've brought
two sausages a piece of cheese
a bottle of wine
drink and eat
wine and bread
light a candle on the altar of the chapel
smoke a cigarette
and rest.
So good so deep so high.
The wind comes in hard gusts
beyond the entrance where I lie
and watch the clouds sailing past
the sky darkens
the stars shine
and I'm filled with a deep calm
a happiness
at being in the world.
There's no other way of putting it and
perhaps I ought to go home now
not flee not travel but settle down
at home.
Perhaps this mountain trek is

the beginning
of the journey home.

Sunday the twenty-seventh of April: Rest day.
Sunday is rest day
but the day doesn't rest
how can it Sunday
rests in its name
but the day doesn't rest
it's nameless.
You're nameless too
in your room at the pension in La Colombe
you're called Don't Do Anything Today
you could be called anything at all
you're called Listen to the Birds in the Bushes
you're called Church Bells Ringing
you're called Women's Voices from the Kitchen
you're called Dog Barking
you're called Lie in Bed and Read
you're called Sun Glowing On the Curtain
you're called Smell of Newly Filtered Coffee
you're called Music on the Portable Radio
you're called Rest Day
you're called Sunday
you're called Loss
you could be called anything at all
it's a long time since anyone has spoken your name.

On Monday I take a bus from La Colombe
to Avignon then the train

to Nice then the train
to Arles where I pay a visit to my publishers
Actes Sud
who've published *Marcher* and *Lettre
Contre l'art* and now *Contre la nature*
which I read from that evening
in the bookshop which is full.
It's strange
being so alone
among so many people
in Arles.
On Tuesday morning
I walk out of the town following
the river along the road
dressed in a black suit white shirt
dirty boots suddenly I'm in the middle of a small
gypsy encampment beneath the trees by the river
four caravans and cars parked
as a shelter or boundary
around the site
so alien
so beautiful
so different
to the place I've just left.
A man is standing in the doorway
of one of the caravans he's
dressed in a black suit a dark
wide-brimmed hat
he calls out a greeting
raises his hand to his hat

as if we both are strangers
he and I.
How good to walk
along the river along the road
which runs parallel to a disused railway
I walk along the line stepping on the sleepers
bolted between the rails
which run straight ahead uninterrupted
to what to where
to something as yet unseen
or heard these grasshopper creakings
wood pigeon wing-clappings frog alarms
along the iron way
these butterfly lift-offs bee movements
from flower to flower
between the rails.
Steel and grass copper and water
sun and iron bending gently now
towards the cloud of crows above the rubbish dump
this smell of the discarded
this smell of something new
the forest tang river air a new girlfriend
how would she smell I
love the smell of sweat
love the smell of the discarded
love the smell of walking.
Walking away from or
walking towards it's
all the same.
Where are you going

when you're not going anywhere
when you just want to go away
if you're really going away
where will you go
d'you know where you're going
or are you going away
to come home?
What is where is home
is it where you live
or is it another place
an unknown place
where you belong?
Can you live in New York
can you live in Berlin
can you live in a forest
do you really want to live in the country
in an old farmhouse
with a new love
or alone
with a dog?
Do you want to live by the sea
or close to a river
do you want to live in a valley
or up a mountain
perhaps on a ridge
with a view of the fjord
or would you rather live in a block of flats
with children
or alone
among other people's children

perhaps you want to live quite apart
on an island
well
where do you want to live
where will you live
where can you live
when you don't love any more?

I'm walking towards a new town
following the old railway track
overgrown
with thistles scrub a dense shrubbery
relieved only by tunnels derelict stations
these railway lodgings
which stand empty.
Dead houses dead homes.
No lights.
Just the sun which is sinking now.
It's starting to get dark and
I must find a place to sleep
go down to the river
find a patch of grass beneath trees
gather twigs and driftwood
build a fire tear up a newspaper
light the fire and lie down
on my pack spread my jacket across my chest
take a nip or two of spirits smoke a cigarette
and fall asleep wake up fall asleep again and
wake up all night.

(Could you hear
the train that rushed
past in your
dreams?)

I take the train for the final stretch
into Montpellier
where I've been invited
to a literary festival
breakfast in the restaurant car
a baguette with brie a bottle of red wine
coffee a glass of Calvados
get off the train drunk
and find my hotel in the middle of
town. It's a fine hotel
with an old lift or elevator
should I say elevator up
to my room on the third floor
a dark room with heavy curtains
a double bed and a writing table
a bathroom with a bath.
I fill the bath with hot water.
Take off my suit and boots
my dirty shirt underwear and socks
and get into the bath.
It's as if the sweat and dirt
is peeled from my body
as if I'm undressing for the second time
and sinking naked into the hot water.

Drink a bottle of cold beer.
Lie in the water and become transformed.

Shed my hair and beard.
My skin loosens from my body.
Fingers shrink nails fall off.
Penis turns grows inside out like a fungus.
Insides visible blood vessels heart lungs liver
spleen floating above my skeleton which is soft
shoulder blades ribs hips kneecaps mashed
together in a clump of yellow wax a foetus
joined by an umbilical cord to the woman's body
which unfurls in the bath.
My mouth fills with water.
Is she drowning?
She's losing her breath choking with water
the water runs into my lungs and I come round
sit up in the bath and wail
like a child.

Drink the bottles from the minibar
first gin then vodka then whisky
smoke cigarettes out of the window
sit at the writing table and write
the introduction to what I shall read
from *Against Nature* written
to a lover I no longer possess.
The only sentence I produce
on the hotel paper is this question
which isn't a question so what is it then

an accusation a prayer a cry for help:
How should one live.
Here the sentence trails off turns white turns dark
before finding its continuation:
without love.
Is that all?
Is that all I'm able to write?
Without love.
How should one live.
Or:
How should one live.
Without love.
That's all I'm able to write.

That evening that night
after my reading
I meet Aurélie Torres she's
in the bar drinking gin says that she works
for the festival as a designer she's the one who
chose the photo of me
for the festival catalogue: And now here you are
she says. You look better in the photograph
she says but then they all do. You don't look
too bad in the flesh either she says
she says she's a Spaniard domiciled in France
in Montpellier for the time being I'm a storyteller
she says. She has a black jacket
white blouse black trousers black long hair
a thin face wide red-lipsticked mouth
deep voice almost masculine no a husky

woman's voice: I'll tell you a fairy tale
she says. Once upon a time in
a small village in the far south of Spain
there lived a little boy called Jesús. He
had fair curly hair which had been bleached
by the sun by the wind by the sea-salt which blew
through the streets between the houses in the little
village where the small boy always
felt himself a stranger even though he made friends
with the animals. He knew the cats in the street
and the stray dogs further out he knew the pigs
on the farms and the horses which he talked to
and fed with carrots for one day he would
ride away on one of the horses through the forest
across the mountains far away to another land
where there were friendlier people who didn't
know him. He didn't know himself
small breasts had begun to develop on the little
boy's chest and his bottom became rounder
with each passing day with each passing year
it just got worse and worse or better and
better he didn't know what to think
about himself and the metamorphosis he was undergoing.
He'd have liked to be a tree or a flower
or a bird yes anything but this
double thing he was he was two
he wanted to be one he was everybody
he wanted to be nobody he wanted to go away
he wanted to die and rise again
if not here then there he thought and

he had no fear of death
he was thirteen by then.
She lights a cigarette.
Shall we dance she asks.
What happened I ask.
Jesús didn't die she says.
He rode away from the village when he was sixteen
through the forest across the mountains far away
to another country where he became a different person
she says.

We dance.
Want me to come along to your hotel room
she says I'm unable to say no we
can drink the wine from the minibar I've got
some cocaine it's good for your prick
she says I'll tell you a fairytale
I say and together we walk out into the town
through the town
she and I.

Thursday the first of May: I don't think anything is more beautiful in a film
in a film
than when food is being prepared
the actual cooking
the skill the kitchen utensils and
the hands working.
Fowls being plucked
the breasts cut off
the legs parted from the carcase

the wings cut off
and fried in a pan with oil
or butter.
And the dessert
the ingredients being mixed
sugar eggs milk
this simple purity
which is folded together
in the correct careful way
in preparation for a
caramel pudding.
This is a scene from Pedro Almodóvar's
Volver
where Raimunda has taken over a restaurant
and is making dinner for the crew
who've just been wrapping up a film
we see the preparations for the meal
in the kitchen
and the high point in *Volver*
for me
is the moment when a pair of hands
place the form containing the refrigerated
caramel pudding
on the work surface and lay a plate
on top of the form turn the form upside down
this TURNING-ROUND-MOVEMENT which reveals
the finished pudding
on the dish
is a moment of magic a conjuring trick
or sleight of hand which makes me catch

my breath as I see the quivering pudding
that becomes motionless on the plate
before it's sliced up
and eaten.
May Day
is associated in my mind
with communal activity. The day
has often commenced with a shared breakfast
during my childhood with my grandparents
in Michael Krohnsgate
in adult life with friends in Øvregaten
where ten or twelve of us congregate around
a table laid in the living room.
We first come together in the kitchen
prepare straightforward dishes
scrambled egg strips of smoked salmon
smoked ham asparagus liver pâté and
freshly baked bread we
drink wine and talk all at once
while we work in the kitchen
women and men
some of us are gays and some lesbians
some are actors others are writers
and parents the children crawl around the kitchen floor
or run in and out of the doors
the way children do run through rooms
on the first of May.
Some of us smoke cigarettes
on the balcony
some cry some laugh

some talk about new lovers
and friends who've died
since we last met. We carry
the food to the table in the living room
which has places laid with glasses and plates
and under the plates are copies
of the song we shall sing
before we eat we sing: *Arise ye workers from
your slumber. Arise ye prisoners
of want* and more tunefully now
twice:
*So comrades come rally
And the last fight let us face. The
Internationale unites the human race*!
Then we eat. It's ten o'clock.
We are a fellowship an intoxicated fellowship now
we must find a slogan and a placard is laid
on the floor Ulla and Kjersti who are lovers
write in red lipstick
on the white cardboard: I think
that people who work with art culture people
etc. should get more money.
We all go out into the city gather
on Torgallmenningen and search for a key slogan
we can all walk behind we quickly agree
on a FREE PALESTINE and join the march.
We walk. We march. We demonstrate.
We shout. We sing. We greet friends
acquaintances the sun shines it rains we
feel the power that fills a mass of marching

people we are filled with the power
of change.
We want to change
we want to have change
a just society
more equal pay
equality for men and women
no discrimination against minorities
no xenophobia
no oil exploration in the north
down with poverty
down with capitalism
accept the refugees
from Syria Iraq Afghanistan Kurdistan
Ethiopia Eritrea Somalia Nigeria
the Ivory Coast these strangers
aren't strangers
they're our friends
today
the first of May.

I have breakfast with Aurélie
in the breakfast room at the hotel
in Montpellier. The literary festival is over
and I'm to take the train to Barcelona
where I'll meet my father
before we check in to the cruise ship
Liberty of the Seas
which will take us on a Mediterranean
cruise from Barcelona to Naples.

But today we'll celebrate
the first of May says Aurélie
as we drink champagne
and eat oysters
in the breakfast room.
The Scandinavian writers
who've been the principal guests at the festival
sweep past our table in light suits and
dark dresses it's as if we're eating breakfast
in a novel by Thomas Mann
or Marcel Proust
in Lübeck or at The Grand Hotel in Balbec
where the white spring light shines
in through the great windowpanes and the patio door
on to the garden and the promenade glows
in the distance. Tonight there's the big
end-of-festival party says Aurélie first there'll be
a dinner here at the hotel and then there's a dance
and bar in the festival marquee all night long
it'll be wonderful she says I'd like
you to stay with me a few days and then
I'd like to visit you in Bergen I've never been to
Scandinavia and I've always longed to see the north
she says. Yes I say that would be nice.
I'm due a month's holiday when the festival is
over I can fly from Nice to Bergen once you've
got home from the trip with your father and then
we can travel around Norway I'd so like to see
your country wouldn't that be lovely she says.
Well yes that would be nice I repeat. Can you

order a bottle of white wine I say I'm
a little unwell it must be the oysters I
must go up to my room to the toilet
it won't take long I'll be back
soon then we'll share the wine I say and
get up from the table walk slowly out
of the breakfast room towards the lift take the lift up
to the third floor let myself into my room
and stuff all my clothes toiletries books
into my backpack put on my jacket and
hurry out of the room run down
the stairs to reception leave the entry card
in my jacket pocket I still have one night
paid for at the hotel walk calmly past
the reception and out through the sliding doors into
the street turn left towards the station.
I sprint towards the railway station.
I bound up the steps to the departure hall
run to the ticket machine and buy
a ticket on the first southbound train
out of Montpellier.

At twelve fifteen I'm sitting on the train
in the restaurant car drinking wine and
deciding to get drunk.
There's nothing better than being inebriated
on a fast train at such high speed racing away
from everything you've done as a stranger
in a strange city it's almost
as if you'd never been there I say

aloud and drink some wine
write in my notebook I'm back
to normality writing and drinking
on a journey on the train
the first of May
under way
to or from
it makes no difference
it's good to be on the move
it's good to be nobody.

I meet my father on Saturday
at the harbour just outside town.
He's arriving on one of the many coaches
that draw up at the parking zone
with thousands of passengers
who all look like my father
women and men they're all alike
that's how it looks from where I'm standing
waiting
outside the embarkation hall.
Who out of all these fathers
and mothers is my father?
Is it the woman with the white sun hat
the dark glasses
the shorts
the sandals
the handbag
is it the man with the yellow sun hat
the dark glasses

the light-blue T-shirt
the shorts
the sandals?
There's several hundred of him and
for a moment I'm sure I've lost
my father he's missing
among this crowd of fathers and
in an instant it hits me that my father will
die.
For the first time it's clear to me
that my father will die I've had
the thought before but it's only been a thought
now here in this mass of people
I feel scared at first then distraught then suddenly
overwhelmed with sadness that he's gone.
On the quayside in Barcelona
I'm paralysed by the thought that my father
will die I can't see him I can't find him
in this mass of tourists boarding
a cruise ship
we arranged to meet at the door
of the embarkation hall
but he's not here
and finally I find my mobile phone
dial his number and wait.
Then I hear him on the phone
and I can tell from the distant voice
which is unrecognizable
on this poor connection
that he's far away

I can hear death I can
hear he's dead.

My father is dead I'm
speaking to him on the phone.

Where are you I shout.

I'm here he says.

Where's here I ask.

Here's here he says.

Is my mother your wife there I ask.

Yes he says.

Is your mother my grandmother there I ask.

Yes he says.

Is my wife your daughter-in-law there too I ask.

Yes he says.

What are you all doing I ask.

We're not doing anything. We're together he says.

You're together I ask.

We're together together he says.

What does that mean I ask.

I can't explain it to you. When you come
here we'll be together too he says.

Together together I ask.

That's it he says.

But where are you I ask.

I'm here he repeats.

Where's here I say infuriated now
like the father who's angry with a son
he's been frightened of losing
and whom he finds without
being able to display any joy
he shows only irritation and anger
at the sight of his missing son I'm
standing by the door in front of the embarkation hall
the dead voice says
and now I realize that he
must be standing at the other end
of the hall I walk quickly round
the building and there is my father
in a white sun hat white T-shirt
light shorts a black suitcase on wheels
in one hand his mobile phone in the other.
I see you you
can ring off I say
tetchily and frustrated too
that I'm unable to show
any pleasure at seeing him
it's been a long time
since I last saw him.
We hug each other.

I love my father but
I'm hardly

ever able to show how fond
I am of him usually I'm
either irritated or angry
on the occasions I do see him perhaps
that's because he's become old
and frail I can't bear to see
my father becoming more and more
helpless I can't bear to see
my father gradually turning into
my son.

I can't bear the way my father's
become dependent on me
just as I was dependent on him
when I was his son
and now I realize that I'm no longer
his son that I've become the one
he's dependent on
a reluctant father to my father
who's getting younger and younger
with the years.

It makes me think back to
the time I lived with his mother
and the way she always spoke of him
as a small child. She always
told stories about my father as a small
boy of my own age often younger
so that even as an eight- or nine-year-old
I was already older than my father.

My father
was that little boy
she always said that poor little
boy Eivind
she spoke to me as an eight- or nine-year-old
of poor Eivind and I
always felt sorry for my father
as an eight- or nine-year-old
that little boy
so often exposed to such
dangers in the street where he lived.
One day from her window in the flat
in Michael Krohnsgate she saw
that poor little boy standing
with two other boys
on a flimsy wooden raft drifting
out of Damsgårdssund
heading out towards the Byfjord
or as she imagined
the open sea she screamed and yelled
from the window but her boy was sailing
helplessly out towards the open sea
where he'd be lost
for ever.

Not long after he could be standing
in the doorway back
from work. He'd
grown into a big man now
tall powerful dark

a beautiful face
sharp blue eyes broken nose
from the boxing he did in his spare time
he worked in a factory and
always came home about four a little
before his wife who was a medical secretary
in what he called a mental hospital
the psychiatric institution that was Dr Martens' Hospital
where my mother worked now he stood in the hall
and hugged his mother
and for several minutes it was impossible for me
to connect this man
with that little boy
who was my grandmother's son
he was her lover her loved one
that was obvious to me as I sat in the kitchen
waiting.
I was waiting for my father.

That old man
with his white sun hat white bushy eyebrows
a round face almost
hidden with skin
that large heavy body almost
immobile taking small steps
as if he's afraid of falling
when he walks as if he's about to fall
bent forward
his arms ready to meet the asphalt
a step by step battle with the ground with

the fall which keeps him upright
that poor big man
boarding the ship
to sail away on the open sea
without a mother without his wife.
Is he still my father?

We're given a cabin on deck eleven
take the lift up and find our way
through the corridors to a reasonably large
light-blue room with a balcony
and bathroom bath washbasin
with golden taps blue towels
dressing gowns slippers a wardrobe
in the small lobby which opens into a little
lounge with a coffee table and sofa mirror
and writing table beneath the flat-screen TV against the
double bed
we'll be sleeping in the same bed
my father and I.

Sunday is rest day quiet day nowhere day
we sail through something blue an all-pervading blue colour
which might be sky or sea
which might be the crossing from blue to blue
an endless journey through immobility and sleep.
Will the journey never end
it hasn't begun
it may be a journey
without beginning or end.

The journey is tedious
the tediousness is infinite and good.

We sleep. We sail.

It's Sunday or Monday
we're having breakfast in a large bright dining room
coffee eggs white bread butter bacon orange juice
cheese grapes half an apple strawberries another cup
of coffee over the loudspeaker system the captain announces
that there are three thousand nine hundred and sixty-three
passengers on board.
The Greek captain says that there
are twenty-seven nationalities on board.
The crew numbers four hundred and seventy-eight
women and men.
There's an ice rink in the bowels of the ship
the ice-dancers are from Russia and the Ukraine.
The ship has three swimming pools
the largest is a children's pool there are hardly
any children aboard.
On the uppermost deck there's a running track
with red rubber underlay which forms an elongated
circle round the ship.
It's a lovely ship.
There's a gym at the front of the ship
on deck eight the place has large windows
giving on to the horizon there's a boxing ring
at the back of the suite.

Two saunas. A beauty parlour.

A shopping arcade. Cafes. Restaurants. Auditorium
Cinema. Disco. Casino. Nightclub.

There's a city aboard the ship.

It's not a beautiful city.
We don't miss the parks the gardens the trees we
miss nothing.
The city sails on towards other cities.
Marseille La Spezia Naples.
We sleep. We eat.
Dinner is served at eight thirty
it's the second sitting
we sit at a Scandinavian table
a couple from Iceland a couple from Denmark
a couple from Sweden my father and me
we are a couple.

We're all nameless we
say our names
and then forget them.

Our table is in the middle of the big dining room
which is surrounded by a gallery
on which are several tables with diners
a wide staircase leads up to the gallery
and on a wide landing half-way up sit
two musicians playing classical music.
The waiters are dark-skinned they're dressed in black
and white.

We eat. We converse.
The music tonight is Haydn and Mozart.
We drink white wine and red wine.
We have cognac with the coffee and dessert
my father drinks whisky.
I fall in love with the Icelandic woman
who's sitting on my left
on her left is her husband
he's younger than me.
His name is Bjarni or Sigurd
she's called Erla María.
She's wearing a pale-blue low-cut dress
white skin blonde hair blue eyes.

After dinner my father and I take
the stairs to the casino on deck seven
there's a bar in among the gaming tables and
machines we sit at the bar
drinking gin and tonic smoking cigarettes.
There are some Russian girls at the bar
one of them says to my father in broken
English are you travelling with your brother?
My father's smoking John Player's.
On his left hand he wears three rings on two
fingers his engagement ring his wedding ring
and a Freemason's ring.
He smokes with his left hand drinks
with his right a perfect harmony between
the hands as if he's embracing
himself.

The Russian girl asks my father where
his wife is. My wife is dead he says
it sounds as if he's just that minute
killed her.

My father's beautiful when he's drinking.
The big hands the rings the glass the cigarettes
the jowly face which turns sharper harder
there's a glint in the eye a light or an earnestness
as if the alcohol's a priming fuel that ignites
the temper inside him he's almost dangerous again he
says: All my life I've loved just one
woman.

My father's only saying things I already know
and yet
this sentence jolts me like one of the blows
from his right hand.
My father and I are in the process of turning into
the same person.

He's always been what I shall become.
All my life I've loved just one
woman they're my father's words and
they're Petrarch's words in a letter
to Boccaccio
and as I'd searched for Petrarch's history
I had without knowing it
searched for my father's history
I'd searched for a love story
which I thought was my own.

I'd searched for my father
here he sits
and I hardly see him at all.

I know only too well
why I don't see him
it's because I
resemble him.

We drink. We smoke.

It's Monday Tuesday Wednesday it's May
and we sit at the bar among the gaming tables
and machines the Russians play
the Chinese play the Japanese play
my father and I drink he says: Money
has never interested me.

I've never had any interests.

You boxed I say I boxed he says
because my father boxed just as you
boxed because your father boxed he says.

You studied chemistry I say I remember
nothing about my studies he says apart
from falling in love
with the woman who was to be your mother.

Have you never been with other
women I ask.

No he says.

Never.

You loved your mother I say I loved
my mother the way you loved your mother the way
a son loves his mother he says.

No you loved your mother like a lover
I didn't love my mother I say and
for the first time in many years I see
that terrible glint in his eye
it's as if time falls away from him
and for a mad moment he is back
at the age when he fought he's just about
to lash out I admired her feared her
it wasn't love it was something else
I say.

Non-love he says.
It was non-love I say.
There's a bit of love in that he says.
There is love in that I say.

I never had any spare time my father says
there was my mother and there was your mother
and there were my studies and a job
which I liked and threw myself into then you
came along and later your sister and there was
work and the family and that's how it's
always been he says.

But now you've got time I say.

Yes and to tell you the truth it's hell
he says I miss your mother my love
and I miss work and I miss the family
it's hard being old I can
tell you so now you know he says.

Old age is a living death he says.

Old age is a long sleep he says.

Old age is a great blackness he says.

And now I'm going to tell you a secret he says
I rather like that Icelandic woman
who sits at our table.

Yes I know I say.

We sail past Marseille La Spezia Naples.
At Naples we take a taxi into the city
we see Naples from the back seat of the car
the taxi driver drives fast so fast
that all we see is pedestrians
running cars braking and accelerating
weaving in and out of traffic queues we see
nothing of Naples.

From the boat deck that evening we spot
three whales

they follow the ship blowing
until they're swallowed up by the sea.

From the boat deck that evening we spot
a plastic dinghy loaded
with people crammed together in the boat
with its outboard motor.

That evening it's the captain's dinner
in the dining room the guests are dressed
up the men in dark
suits or dinner jackets the women in
party dresses the tables have
white tablecloths white linen napkins
the waiters enter in a long line
marching into the dining room they wave
their white napkins over their heads
twirl their napkins in the air
and simultaneously the dinner guests raise
their napkins in the air and wave them
in the same way and there's a white wind
passing through the dining room a white wind
of napkins waving in the air like
a wind of distress or survival
in the beautiful dining room which is sinking
that's how it feels
we are the ones sinking
for several minutes we
wave the white napkins above our heads
four or five hundred white napkins

which fill the air of the overflowing dining room
it's so lovely
that I begin to cry.

The orchestra plays the chandeliers sparkle
the rustle of silk and jewellery a gentle
hum of voices that rises and falls
in time to the movement of hands with knife
and fork there's salmon pâté as a starter
with white wine red wine with the lamb
my father flirts with Erla Maria he's
slicked his hair with water shaved
put on a dark suit white shirt black
tie gold-rimmed glasses a seventy-eight-year-
old gentleman he raises his glass
and proposes a toast to the ladies
at our table he begins to get tipsy
and as always he's altered by the alcohol
he becomes sharper bolder the alcohol
transforms him from something old
into something terribly young
this old man turns into
a seducer his hair reassumes
its former dark lustre the skin
on his face stretches the wrinkles smooth out
the colour returns to his cheeks and his lips
fill with blood become fuller a sensual mouth
which drinks the wine and spits out the words
he becomes a master of words
a master of conversation my father

concentrates on Erla Maria
forgets his age forgets his son
and all the formalities that exist
at a dinner table I kick
his leg under the table and now I discern
moisture forming on his spectacles
as if bad weather is brewing there
above his face thunder and lightning
if I'm not careful I
kick his leg once more and
the kick completes the transformation
totally now he's no longer my father
but an omnipotent Father of All who at any moment
may turn into anything
a swan
or a bull yes
isn't he already a swan
sitting there beating his wings
stretching his long neck out
across the table towards Erla Maria
a great white swan he wraps his wings
around her and his bird's body covers
the woman's body with feathers and beak wings
and feet I can't see her any more
only the terrible bird
which threatens to devour every one of us
at the dinner table.

Don't I harbour a desire
to be a swan like that too

a white wanton bird
which without warning can cover
any chance woman
without reflection without sympathy
only a leaden white desire
which alights on the chosen one
the most beautiful one
for example at the dinner table
Erla Maria
or another of the women on the cruise ship?
There are lots of them
but I've neither the courage nor the strength
to approach a single one of them
after the
break with Janne I've
lost the ability to love
and even more seriously perhaps I've lost
the life force itself I am a shadow
of myself I'm even a shadow
of my father who every evening
sits at the dinner table and does what I
should do my father orders
a bottle of champagne for our table
it's the last evening of the cruise
we're sailing direct from Naples to Barcelona
I'm just waiting for the seance at the dinner table
to end so that I can haul my father
up to the bar away from the company
but the guests around the table seem to find him entertaining
he's not the problem at our table

it's me
it's me
who's ashamed of my father
and sit there sombre and silent at the table
shamefaced over my father
who toasts in champagne he sings
a Swedish drinking song talks Danish
to the Danish couple and invites himself
to Iceland where he's never been and where
he's always wanted to go next summer
we'll go to Iceland he says and raises
his champagne flute TO SCANDINAVIA he announces
loudly and even this causes me shame
this strident word Scandinavia here among
waiters from the Philippines and
Sri Lanka diners from twenty-seven nations
all talking quietly around their tables and
hearing this dreadful word Scandinavia
ring through the dining room like a declaration of war
almost I cringe
as if someone's beating a tin drum
or blowing a trumpet we clink
glass against glass TO SCANDINAVIA goes the shout
around our table and I feel ashamed
not just of my father but of the entire company
and of myself for taking part in this
luxury cruise in the Mediterranean I see the way
Erla Maria leans across the table
to my father what's the matter with your son

why's he so quiet she whispers HE'S GOT
A BROKEN HEART my father says.

I set out on this trip
with my father because he hardly goes anywhere at all
most weekdays he sits in his small
flat reading the morning paper listening to the radio
watching television and walking the few steps from
the living room
to the kitchen to heat up the dinner that's
delivered to his door. He takes up less and less space
inside the flat as if he's preparing
to disappear entirely. It seems to me that he's
also shrinking into himself from all this inactivity
he crumples up curbs his arm movements
his head seems to sink down between his shoulders he falls
between the living room and the kitchen more and more often
and when I visit he's got scratches and bruises
cuts on his lips a black eye almost
like in the old young days when he was boxing but now
it's the rug he's fighting or items of clothing
lying discarded on the floor more and more often
he goes down flattened by
a pair of slippers which aren't where they're supposed to be.
I visit him and haul him out into
the corridor force him down the stairs and then we take
a short stroll over to the artificial grass pitch
at Stemmemyren where there's usually a football match.
Once a week he has to walk all the way from his flat
up to the house where I live I make him dinner

every Thursday and if he doesn't walk up for his dinner
which sometimes happens he blames the rain
the wind a pain in his leg
that he's got a dizzy turn that he feels unwell
but instead he drives up
I see the car from the kitchen window
and he doesn't get dinner that's the rule and
maybe it's hard but I can't bear to see
my father weak can't bear to see him get old
he brings the car and I send him home
without giving him dinner. I
sit alone in the kitchen fuming
because he's broken our agreement sad
because I have to be strict with the old man
and one Thursday when I was sitting alone in the kitchen
eating our dinner
I got this idea that we might go
somewhere together
and because he hardly likes walking at all
I began thinking about going on a cruise
like that he'd be able
for the last time perhaps
to see a few great cities
if only from the deck of the cruise ship.

And here we sit at the dinner table
aboard the *Liberty of the Seas*
during this journey
this week at sea
my father has eaten well slept well

he's gone for daily walks on the jogging track
round the ship's uppermost deck
he's just got fitter and fitter
while I've gone downhill.
It's as if he sucks his strength out of me I
can't sleep at night my appetite's gone
I often feel dizzy and nauseous
irritated and unwell
and I've lost the desire to move about
lie in bed as long and as often as I can
listen to the radio watch television in our little cabin.
Sometimes my father has to force me out of bed
out of the cabin to take the few steps
to the lift we use
to descend to the dining room
I get weaker and weaker
and he becomes stronger
with each day that passes
sometimes when I'm lying next to him
sleepless in bed at night
with wet toilet paper in my ears
I think: He's going to outlive me
my father's going to outlive me I think
at night when he's asleep
and I lie awake
totally exhausted by this journey
of motionlessness and luxury
of tedium and meaninglessness
it's as if I've moved into
a tiny flat in sheltered accommodation

apart from the fact that this flat moves around
it's sailing towards death I think
at night we're sailing through the night
towards death that's what it feels like
on all those sleepless nights aboard the cruise ship.

Saturday the tenth
of May: We fly
from Barcelona to Bergen.
Flying is my least favourite thing
not because I've got a phobia
not because I'm frightened of being killed
but because I've got a real fear of sitting
trapped among people I don't know
in a space it's impossible to get out of.
Several times
during the course of a flight
I'll be about to faint
or have a seizure
I'm convinced my heart will stop
or that I won't be able to breathe
or that I'll burst into tears
or that I'll start shouting
and screaming for help
that I'll hit the person next to me
or claw at her hair
that something terrible will happen
but it doesn't happen I manage
with the greatest effort
to remain in my seat.

I sit completely still and quiet
in my seat but everything inside me is in turmoil
as if the horror of the actual journey
that we're flying through the air
at five hundred miles an hour
has its counterpart in the internal journey
which is lethal now
at any moment my heart will stop
my breathing cease my eardrums burst
my brain be destroyed my sanity be shattered
my soul die
squeezed in here among three hundred passengers
who're reading the newspaper or sleeping
in the semi-darkness high high above the sea
and the mountains down below.
Hell isn't a place
deep beneath the earth's crust
it's a stretch of sky
between departure and arrival.
It follows from this
perhaps
that Paradise is home
at any rate I always vow
in the air that I'll never
travel by plane again.
This notion persists
up to the moment the cabin crew reach my seat
with a trolley
I buy a half bottle of red wine and
a half bottle of white with my food

a miniature of cognac to go with coffee
and a half bottle of sparkling wine with the packet
of cashews and about halfway through
consuming all this I finally
calm down.
A gentle pleasure suffuses my body
from the alcohol how nice to drink
in the air at altitude in the plane to sit
completely still at enormous speed
travelling homeward home
I could almost wish we weren't going so fast
that the journey would last longer
that we could sit like this in the air
in the semi-darkness for as long as possible
how lovely to look out of the window
at the gunmetal-blue of the sea's surface shining
like steel or paper
you can almost read the letters in the waves
a script that suddenly meets the land and becomes painting
is it yellow or brown-turning-to-green
a colour that rises gently into the greyness
which turns white we see there's snow in the mountains
before the plane hurtles into a bank of cloud it
wraps itself gently around the fuselage
you get sleepy want to go to sleep
here in space
it's hardly surprising that the air traveller
thinks about death
as a sleep in a similar sky
here we'll sleep one day

we hope and trust
in a bed of clouds.
We've already begun the descent
we're already on the way down and home
how sad to lose altitude
and fall through clouds which turn to rain
now we see our home-town through a water pattern
on the plastic window we see the city of rain
through a curtain of rain
for a few minutes it's as if we're travelling under water
a submarine journey in grey
before we land.
Each time I return home
from a journey
I'd like to start a new life.
I'd like to move into the same house
as if it were a new house
no big changes
just a number of small changes
they'll make a difference
they'll open up the possibility of a new life
in the old one.
I rearrange the furniture in the living room move lamps
around
push chairs lug the bed from the bedroom
to the guest room wanting to wake up
in a new place with a new view
not so different from the old one
a small dislocation
a small transformation

is what I'm expecting and hoping for
after making changes in the house
but after only a few days
in this new life I slip back into the old
one which is stronger than the new
the new life is daily
swallowed up by the old life and one day
I move about in the new one in the same way
as I inhabited the old one even though everything
is different now that Janne doesn't live
here any more.
It's as if the house doesn't want to forget
it's as if the house doesn't want to change
despite all the alterations I make
inside it. I've
reluctantly
thrown away the clothes she left behind
got rid of her desk and books dumped
the books in a skip put her crockery and
plates into a box and carried them up to the attic
I've removed the photos of her
from my bedside table from my desk from the kitchen wall
but it's as if she's still here
I don't know how long it takes
before someone who moves out
is gone.

Can only a new love
chase the old one out of
the house? I shudder at the thought

of a new woman moving around her rooms
sitting in Janne's place in the kitchen
lying like her on the sofa
that another might lie
next to me on Janne's side of the bed.
I don't want it
I can't do it
I don't want a new lover
in the house and I don't want to move either
I want to live alone
that's what I've decided to do.

It's Monday.

I could happily have married my bed.

My neighbours are arguing, I envy those who've got something
to argue about.

Doors slam, plates smash.

I live off other people's noises.

I'm the perfect spouse.

I've lived alone for almost three years.

We are dependent on noises.

The noises from the city sound like something hostile.

It's May.

Say no, say no.

There are pleasant sounds.

The sound of the wind caressing the trees.

The traffic's beauty.

The traffic as flora.

The beautiful destroying the good.

We excuse ourselves and say: Even nature
destroys nature.

Changes are natural, we say.

The glaciers are melting.

The sound of snow melting, that's beautiful.

Spring, the everlasting spring.

It's always spring here.

Always May.

It's May.

I could have married my arms.

I envy the birds, the birds which pair for life.

Two and two. There are places where you find trees
growing into one another.

It's just a case of standing still, long enough.

It's unnatural to be alone.

July is no longer July.

My rage is turning into a disease,
that's natural.

Nature is sick too, we notice it with every
month.

January is no longer January.

February is no longer winter.

It's May here, even in October.

The rhododendron is budding for the second time.

The snow melts, that's natural.

It's May.

May is the loveliest month.

I've made up my mind to love Janne as long
as I live.

I don't want the idea of eternal love to
be a thing of the past.

I'm against nature.

I am not me.

I age three years with each year that passes.

I'm reading a book about bees.

I don't fly any more.

I am not you.

A year can encompass a whole life and it can be
utterly empty.

What will I say, what should I say.

She taught me to eat oranges.

I'm the ideal spouse.

The sight of anything yellow can cause me
to break down.

I'm old, very young.

The loneliness you choose is a type of rebellion.

Fruit knife, china side plate, a napkin.

We felt cold and we ate oranges.

What should I say, what will I say.

It was summer, perhaps autumn, perhaps spring.

I'd fallen in love with her loneliness.

May is the yellow month.

The full moon in May, that's a killer.

The crocus comes up out of the ground, buds,
flowers, first the yellow, then the violet,
then the white.

The daffodils bloom. The tulips.

Everything is yellow and painful.

Everything goes on, without us.

That's good.

∾

May, that year, was the hottest month
ever recorded in B.

We had this feeling of being happy.

We had this feeling of living at the other
end of the continent.

South, far north.

I thought we'd be a couple for evermore.

How will I live without you?

There's nothing so soothing as walking
over roots and pine needles, under conifers in
dappled sunlight.

White anemones in clumps, on the edge of the copse,
it hurts to walk out of a wood.

People die and change the seasons.

The summer came, followed by a long, warm
winter.

The sight of just one lemon can cause me
to break down.

I'm young, very old.

My favourite colour is pink.

I'm the ideal spouse.

I'd have liked to marry a man.

The seasons changed, perhaps they're disturbed.

When the bees disappear, what is it the end of?

We alter the seasons.

The sky is cloudless.

The cherry trees are flowering.

The beggars have taken up their fixed places, like
sculptures, sitting, kneeling.

A man passes by, dressed in a grey suit, white
shirt, his mobile phone clamped to his ear.

Most of us don't see what we see.

It's impossible to understand the colour blue.

I'd like to write a history of colours.

Kamilla has a knitted sweater the same colour
as her hair. The name of the colour is Kamilla-black.

Janne-blue. Kamilla-black. Christel-white.

Sun-red. Polluted.

The end colour is yellow.

Can we replace the bees?

Our silence is our politics.

Our passivity is a sad activism.

We're children for as long as we can be, until childhood
is taken away from us.

We're children who steal childhood.

We're thieves, it can be proved each and every day.

We cut down trees. We steal oil.

We eat other people's food.

We get others to commit the crimes for us.

We get people with nothing to steal for us.

We get people with nothing to kill for us.

We get people with nothing to make war for us.

We get people with nothing to die for us.

Kamilla phones and says I'm a thief.

You steal love.

I was never a good brother to my sister.

Little sister is a lovely expression.

The dandelion unfurls in a meadow of buttercups, yellow overshadowing yellow.

Can one say that the forest moves?

Janne read Shakespeare wearing sunglasses.

Her hand stroked my head in the same way as it stroked her dog.

She preferred having breakfast alone.

She didn't like being ordered about.

She didn't like rain.

She could hit hard when she got angry.

She never bought anything of poor quality.

She never had much money.

She was in love, but something wasn't right.

She was writing a novel.

She had everything, but something or other was missing.

She had a protective arsenal of clothing, woolly hats, scarves, sweaters, jackets, coats, cloaks.

She hid inside her clothes.

She undressed as if it were a display.

A display of nakedness.

A display of loneliness.

A girl who reads is a girl already lost.

It's Sunday.

Sleeping is an art.

The dreams of the dead, perhaps that's us.

We dream of the dead as if they're alive.

The dead are alive. It's the truth the dead know.

We don't treat the dead well.

Will she once again lie down next to me
in bed and say she's yearning to make love. That's
something only she and my sleep know.

When we sleep, we make love to the dead.

It's May. It's November.

The solar eclipse made Kamilla leave her
husband and daughter.

She's a person who makes her most important decisions
in the dark.

She always phones at night.

Some relationships play out between two voices
on the phone.

At night. In the darkness of the phone. The voice says.
You're a man who steals love.

This distance, he says, is the closest we
come to each other.

It's the closest we come to love, he
says.

He loves her voice.

May moves towards April or June.

Life without love can be good, but it has no pleasures.

The sky is cloudless.

A young man without clothes.

Can one say that nature is getting dressed?

Undressing is a lonely business.

Loneliness in May is cruel.

Write a letter. Send it to Emily Dickinson.

We're ruining the seasons.

A report about flowers.

A letter about species that no longer exist.

Send the letter to your daughter.

I'm the perfect spouse.

I love the house I live in.

Sometimes I wake up as a woman.

I'm three years older with each year that passes.

Loneliness isn't something that comes easily.

Nakedness is generally painful.

Nature shows its wounds.

Write down the entire day's meteorological observations.

The title of a book that'll never be written:
Love Between Men Who Love Women.

A boy who reads, is a boy already lost.

Kamilla's bathing costume is yellow.

A shoreline. Sea rocks.

Blue sea.

We swim, sweat.

Make love under water.

Hold tight to love.

We're swimming with children who drown.

AUTUMN

What did I hear on the news today I almost couldn't hear it
the coffee maker roared gurgled this machine
that sucks up water through a tube forcing
the water from the reservoir and out along a metal arm which
releases it drop by drop dripping over the coffee even the
first drop gives off a strong aroma a coffee smell
that fills the kitchen on the morning of the first of
October I heard the news today oh boy a boat load of
refugees more than five hundred they say capsized
off the coast of Lampedusa.
Up to a hundred and ninety-eight
they don't know the precise number
how can one count the drowned
how can one count the dead
when they're drowning in hundreds in thousands
off the coast of the lovely island of Lampedusa.
The newsreader says that the sea has become a graveyard
for refugees I can hardly hear her over the din
of the coffee maker the water gurgling a spurting
stream or frothing sea if you put your ear right
up close to the jug you can almost hear the dead.
The nameless black Odysseus is drowned without native land
without new land without discoveries other than his demise
on the first of October.

The first cup of coffee tastes good.
The trees have already begun to shed their foliage
the lawn is covered with leaves
as if autumn were a carpet
nature spreads over summer.
It's sunny today Wednesday the first of October
starlit full moon so light at night
brighter light during the day
almost white during the day a white hard light
which shines through the crowns of the trees the green yellow brown
leaves lose colour and assume a heaviness or lightness
which loosens the stalks from the bough and there at this
moment now the leaf falls it rocks
twirls in the light turns in the wind it falls
towards the grass.
We should have watched that together.
The sparrows fly in and out of the foliage it's
impossible to make them out in the trees bird breasts and wings
have the same speckled colour as the autumn leaves another
leaf falls is that a sparrow flying up
no it's impossible to tell one from the other
it's you and I who are so far from each other
this autumn.
The second cup of coffee tastes good.
What's the difference between the first and second of October?
There's no difference they're the same day
the same day every single day
without you.
By tomorrow the number of dead

drowned will have increased to three hundred and twenty they say
and the day after more than thirty more
dead
women and children men and men some of them can't be
separated they clasped each other in the water
and sank
I can hardly hear it
only a few hundred yards from the beach at Lampedusa
they say it's whispered they shout
above the rumble of the coffee maker in the kitchen
where I sit listening
to the news over my breakfast.
The leaves are falling from the trees soon
they'll stand there naked just outside the kitchen window
the lawn is covered with leaves
as if autumn is a piece of cloth
nature has drawn over the dead.

It's October Thursday the second of October
the first October rain falls first gently
not audible or even visible until the windowpane is
misted covered with small pearls of water which gather get heavy and
run in stripes down the glass transparent sketches
they draw a new view a new tree a new hedge new
streets new houses dissolving
a new day.
Then it rains heavily
so hard that it's impossible now to tell the rain
from the trees the rain from the houses the rain from the streets the rain
from the day

a day of rain.
Every Thursday my father comes to dinner
every Thursday I look forward to this visit
which often disturbs my equilibrium my composure my
day which I've worked so hard to make
like other days.
To place the day in the right proportion to other days
to organize the day into a beginning and end
that's natural that follows the light that follows
common sense that follows the seasons the months the weeks
that follows the days and the day
demands a lot
almost all my strength and effort.
I could wish things were different
that I could follow the days
the way they slip away
without me.
My father is seventy-eight and not good on his feet
he isn't mobile enough sits still too much
in the tiny flat he lives in
so we have an arrangement that he'll walk
the few hundred yards from his home up to my place
when I'm making dinner
for him
that's our agreement
but often he'll drive up
because it's raining or windy or because it's
cold he's always got some excuse
to take the car not walk

and this breach of our agreement
can seriously affect my composure
I really have to concentrate on not becoming furious
not ruining the dinner that he's already
ruined by driving his car
to our dinner date
and today's is to turn into a terrible dinner
one of the very worst
because he comes driving
with winter tyres on
in October.
He's had his car fitted with studded tyres
on Thursday the second of October
I spot the car from the kitchen window
open the window and hear a totally new noise
from the car the wheels drumming on the asphalt
a hard brutal sound against the wet asphalt
on a lovely October day
it isn't winter isn't cold isn't frosty isn't icy
it's mild and rain-sodden
a normal October day
it's October today
I'm close to breaking down.

What is a day
what's it made up of
what does it look like? My father is dead
living dead
where is he?

He was sitting at this dining table yesterday
a ghost I'm sure that I saw him that I
heard him or was it his shadow that sat in the kitchen
eating. He said: It could begin snowing at any time.
He said: It's got colder at night. He said: I'm
cold.
My father's cold
he's frozen fast in old age and cold
motionless congealed hidden in rime beneath ice
I understand now what he tries to say
every Thursday:
Your father's dead
he's trying to tell me that my father's dead.

When my father came through the door
expectant
because of the smell of dinner
in a good mood
because he'd managed to get the car tyres changed
he encountered an angry son
so angry that I was close to hitting him
I had to use all my willpower to keep my
hands down why the hell have you changed
to winter tyres studded tyres in October I yelled
at the old man
so loudly that he stepped back and raised his hands
in defence: It'll rain the whole of October
the whole of December the whole winter apart from a few weeks
in January or February and today it's the second of October

it's raining it's pouring with rain
I shouted at my father.
There's no dinner
it's cancelled you've broken our agreement the agreement is that   you
must walk here it's about the only walk   you
get during the whole   week   you
sit there the whole day damn it the whole week   you
you hardly get up at all and your legs are starting
to waste away you're hardly able to walk and   you
are   seventy-eight   you
and now I started   crying   you
aren't old enough to wither away like this.

My father
I shoved him out of the door
surprised at my own fury it welled up
and wouldn't subside got worse wilder
as if it was death I was struggling against
the weak death
the cowardly death
the slow idiotic death
which my father had chosen
for himself and his son.

My father
shook his great body
with its broad shoulders big hands
that once could have knocked anyone down
he shook with rage
I shoved him out of the door

pummelled and pushed with all my might
as if I were trying to push him back in time
and in a few furious seconds I saw that he'd recovered
his balance I pushed him back
to the age I wanted him to be
I struck and he struck back
a punch
so beautiful and fast
that his hand crashed through a wall of time
and landed on his son's face.

When I was a boy when I was young
when I grew up
there was no one I looked up too and admired
more than my father.

Fighter ladykiller the academically gifted son
of working parents he was my hero
and more than that
he became my best friend my father
there was nothing I wanted more
than to be like him and now here he stood
in the doorway so burdened with age and troubles
I couldn't bear the sight
of resignation and death
this father without authority
like old Lear
completely helpless
a fool in the doorway
in the dusk in the evening rain on a day

in October the wind ruffling his silver-grey hair
which plastered itself to his pate in the wet which
seeped through his clothes and he was soaking
the wind jostled him back and forth in the twilight
he opened his arms as if seeking protection
from his son's injustice
from the storm's harshness
from life's coldness he was cold
cold and homeless he stood outside
the door
a superannuated dad an unkempt harbinger:
Your father's dead he said.

How will the son manage
without his father?
Perhaps the worst thing is to watch death circulate
in the guise of a father
who trembles who trips who falls
who stands at the door
with a cut on his nose bruises
under his eyes a bleeding wound on his forehead
because he's tripped on the corner of a rug
and fallen flat on the living room
floor bashed his face on the floor
knocked down by a rug.
And perhaps most difficult of all:
the son is like the father.
The son can be knocked out by a rug too.
Father and son drink

they have that in common
and now the father is outside the door
with a battered face
his face marked by alcohol
is that the face you wear
when you come to dinner with your son?
And you show a similar face
to your father at the door?
You who want to be like your father
you are your father's like.
Is that why you're so enraged
so disappointed for both your sakes?
For a moment you want to go out on to the steps
and embrace the old man
but you don't do it you push him away
push him further down the gravel path
you want him to take himself off home
to his death so that you can be left in peace
with yours you close the door close your eyes
stand a while in the lobby
unable to cry you're too incensed
so angry and upset that you simply must
go into the kitchen and open a bottle of gin.
The bottle's empty.
There should be another bottle
somewhere in the kitchen cupboard
behind the floor-mopping pail with the cleaning liquid
and the bottle of bleach among the detergents
and the empty bottles under the sink yes there

rolled up in a cloth at the back of the cupboard
almost hidden in the cupboard is a whole bottle
of vodka
unopened.

My father's lived alone
for nearly seventeen years. Seventeen years
without love
without any love other than the one
he still harbours for the deceased.
He's never managed never wanted to
meet another woman
he's wanted to be together with his late wife
as long as he lives.
He met her as a fifteen-year-old
and remained with the same woman
for forty-eight years while she lived
seventeen years after she died
a lifelong love affair
not unlike Petrarch's relationship with Laura
first the living Laura
and later the dead Laura
whom Petrarch loved just as much
if not more
than the young Laura
just as we love the dead
more than she who lived
just as we love the one who's forsaken us
more than her we lived with

just as we love the one who's gone
more than any other we meet
and love
without being able to love
that was Petrarch's love
that is my father's love
and my own.
It may be that I've inherited my father's disease
I think in the kitchen
the disease of love.

Awake to a storm the house shaking can you say
that a house trembles?
Great gusts buffet the bedroom window
the veranda doors in the living room the windows buckle
inwards will they shatter?
As if someone's trying to move the house
push it away.
But the house stands.
The house stands on a hill above the fjord sheltered
from the sea by islands and mountains a poor defence
against the wind it blows through the house.
The timbers of the house breathe the windowpanes
screech can you say that a house struggles?
If the house lives
I'm fearful
that the house's heart
will be broken
by the powerful wind.

Extreme weather has got a name
it's called Destruction.
It's Friday the third of October
and the storm is stopping planes and cars
closing bridges
sinking boats
bringing down phone lines
blacking out television channels
cutting off the internet
darkening homes
for a few hours
we live
in an ideal world.

Until the power comes back on again
and the news invades the kitchen
which smells of freshly brewed coffee toast
a ten-year-old girl
goes to the market in a town
in northern Nigeria
under her dress is a vest
someone has put on her
as if it was underwear
can one imagine those hands
dressing the little girl
before she heads off to market
one Friday morning
those black hands
that hitch the suicide vest to the girl's body

and help the girl pull her dress
over her head over the vest
and propel her
towards the market
no
I am unable to imagine such hands
or the man they belong to
are they his hands
no
they don't belong to him
they belong to an evil which is far greater
than this man who tells the girl
about Paradise.
I switch the radio off
ring my daughter
who's at work in a perfumery
it's barely two years since
the shop she was working in had its windows shattered
by an explosion so violent
that she thought she was going to die
she ran out into the street
frightened for her life
that was in Oslo
Friday the twenty-second of July.
I ring my daughter
to ask if she's doing all right
it's Friday with lots of shoppers in the shopping centre
where she works
there are the same crowds there

as in the market in Nigeria.
Her phone is switched off
presumably she's busy
and I leave a message on her answerphone
I love you
I say.

On Saturday I read in the newspaper
that the ten-year-old girl killed twenty people
in the market.
They suspect that the Islamic army
Boko Haram is behind this suicide bombing
its soldiers have begun to put
explosive vests
on small girls in Nigeria.
I can't help thinking
that the youths who attach the explosives
to the girls' bodies
really do believe in Paradise.
They must believe in Paradise
in a better life
an eternal life
for the girls.
And when they send the girls off to the market
to die
they're sending their girls to Paradise.
I must believe this
I must believe.
These devout young soldiers

force me to believe in Paradise
but what happens to all the people killed who died
with these girls
of ours
where do the victims go
according to these young believers?
Hell exists
these young believers
are right about that.

The wind catches the flowers on the living-room table
blows the heads off the azalea
snaps the gladioli
a flash in the room lightning and thunder
the windowpanes rattle the curtains fan out
into the living room where I'm sitting
with my outdoor jacket on
the old green army jacket
it's wind- and rainproof
the wind blows the sheets on the writing table
across the floor blows the sheets out of order
and chronology yesterday becomes today
today is a day long ago
now her letters are blown off the table.
Where was it she wrote: I've
met someone else. Perhaps
you think it's a bit strange
that he's a friend of yours.
A bit strange yes what should I do

with this terrible rage
that ravages my body
like a tempest yes what should I do
not to break down in the storm.

I close the veranda doors open
a bottle of wine
can one kill out of love?
I really want to destroy
this man who is my friend
your lover.
Over and over again I imagine
how I beat him senseless
or injure him enough to make him get out
of our life
so that it's the two of us again
as before.
Haven't I got the right to injure a friend
who injures a friend?
What is the difference between external
and internal pain?
I'll harm him just as much
as he's harming me
is this unreasonable isn't it justice
really?
I knock back the bottle open
another slower now that the alcohol
has wrapped itself like a damp cloth around my heart
I know perfectly well

that he's a good-looking man.
When I've finished with him he won't
be looking so good
broken nose
split lips
cut face
no front teeth
he'll resemble me
the way I looked
when you met me.

On Saturday the fourth of October I
take the bus into town
to visit the Vinmonopol
go to two different outlets
so that I can buy a bottle of gin
three bottles of wine two bottles of vodka
that should last the weekend
remember
how my father described his visits to the Vinmonopol
as expeditions
to 'the Poles'
understand
exactly what he meant by that
it takes a certain courage
to go into the place with a hangover
to fill your backpack with bottles
greet
the girls on the tills

women you know
better than any other
lady friends
pay
with a card or cash
smile
ashamed of your unfaithfulness
your love
of alcohol.

In town I buy cigarettes
a fashion magazine two books music
by Mendelssohn the motets the psalms
a new grey Nike track suit
I like writing and drinking
in training gear.

In the fashion magazine I read
about the Danish photographer Jan Grarup.
For his thirteenth birthday
he got an Instamatic camera
from his parents
and he took loads of pictures. He's
recently returned from a journey
through the Central African Republic
where with his camera he'd recorded
how Muslims
were hunted down and slaughtered
by the Christian militia
Anti-balaka.

He saw men lying on the side of the road
with their penises
in their mouths.

I promise myself
that I'll beat up your new
lover sometimes violence is necessary
to set limits
and as he won't respect
my warnings my words
I'll beat them into him
word by word
I write
to you.

I flounder feverishly with this letter
which has to make it clear to you
that I'll beat up your lover
first break his nose
he deserves that
and then I'll break
his right arm
that's easy
I'm trained for that sort of thing
press my foot against his arm break it
quickly
it'll be a while before he'll
write again
I write.

Sunday the fifth of October a sleepless night.

Is it the date
that's keeping me awake?
Are you making love tonight?
Is there a full moon?
Is it the letter I wrote and sent?
Do I regret it
or not?
Are you pregnant?
Why aren't I asleep?
Why is there no one here?
Why are you still here?
Is the lamp switched off?
Can I live without love?
Why is it raining so heavily blowing so hard?
Is it nature that's sick?
Is it the world coming to an end?
Tonight?
Am I frightened?
What will I do tomorrow?
The same as I did today?
Is there any point going on living
without you?
Do I need help?
Who is there who can help me?
Am I hearing voices?
Are you whispering?
Are you laughing making love whispering
like we did?
Is he a better man than me?

What's happened to my sleep?
Is it true that what you're both doing is keeping me awake?
That we're still together
even when you're with someone else?
That there's no distance at all
even though you're somewhere else?
Will it be long till morning comes?
When it's morning at last
when he leaves you
and leaves you lying alone in your bed
then it may be
that I'll find sleep.

It's Monday
the first day
of a new week I've always liked Mondays
beginnings a new relationship a new life a new
country a new city now that all this is past and over
I long for the end
the end is definitively something new.
I no longer understand the fear of the end
of death that's obviously a result
of my age I'm fifty-three and have done
all I wanted
what remains to me
perhaps
is to write a book
a last book
about death.

The Final Book
that'll be the title.
Thinking about a new book
always makes me excited
and especially this one
which will be the last.
I want to write a book about death
a good death
the sort that comes when it's supposed to.
Not the death that comes too early
which cuts short a life
not accident not murder not terrorism
not poverty starvation suffering not disease
or the long painful death
Rilke describes in *The Notebook of Malte Laurids Brigge*:
Each has the death that suits him.
Not a romantic death
not a beautiful death
not the mystical death
nor yet the believer's death
which Bach sings about in his cantata
Come, Thou Lovely Hour of Dying.
Not death as a beginning
of a new life
but death as an ultimate end
death that naturally results from a
lived life
the humdrum death

that most of us
die and will die.

I shall equip my home
as a sanatorium
and then I'll go off sick
I'll write the diagnosis on a piece of paper
and place it on the bedside table
in case I don't wake up:
I'm suffering from a broken heart
it's one of the worst things that can happen to
a healthy human being and I require no
treatment.

No longer cut my hair my beard
grows my face shrinks
dries up flakes off
as when a wall begins to crack skin
wrinkles over skin
below my hair which is turning grey
YOU'RE LOSING COLOUR
my sight dims my hearing fails you
fuse like some aged thing
under a soft scarred fleshly material
sewn together stitch by stitch
into an appearance that shrinks
has almost disappeared
in a thick black overcoat
spectacles hat felt wool polyester
acrylic and together in a hoary defence

you hide behind
eyes of glass and water
an empty wet gaze
you don't want to see you don't want to be seen
vanished already into the multitude
of your peers.

Drink off all I have left
of oblivion ah so good
to drink now I recall
everything all the details
my grandmother's pearl earrings my grandfather's boiler suit
filthy from work and tobacco
my maternal grandfather's tailored trousers
his pale right hand blue with ink stains
my maternal grandmother's Jewish nose inherited
by my mother me
my mother's wigs black red
blonde I couldn't recognize her
from the day before my father's beauty
ruined by photographs I've
never seen a more beautiful man the smell
of the poteen he distilled in the cellar
where I sit and write
my sister's birth
that soft bundle a cocoon of pink
laid screaming in my
bedroom
blue I dreamt of bats wars

between colours
always had a fear
of killing
the one lying next to me in bed.

Fear of God
extricated me from the established church
straight after confirmation.
I accepted gifts of money and went
down to the Reverend Freuchen he stammered
divided the scriptures into consonants be-be-begged
me to take the chair on the other side
of the heavy desk took out the church register
with my name
newly inscribed crossed it out
with a biro and ruler two straight lines
through my name and childhood faith you're quite cer-cer-cer-
certain about this he said
and I was off the parish register
unchristian again.

I wrote and read myself remote
from the class that works
and up to the class that dreams
which doesn't need money
to live a fulfilled life
because we know poverty
and do not fear it.
It's the privilege of our class

that even without possessions
without income without money
we're still held in high esteem
in the world of the bourgeoisie
which keeps us alive
and the so-called art we create
because the middle classes need art
and our names
in order to maintain a certain respectability
as a society. The state sends us off
on tours we put up at expensive hotels
eat fine food drink wine in Madrid
in Rome in New York in Copenhagen we
rub shoulders with ambassadors politicians charlatans
cultured women and men
drink eat
shake hands sip champagne grab
canapés munch mumble talk nonsense
to businessmen and women
eat drink
at exclusive restaurants
our bills paid
visit bars in Oslo
in Trondheim in Stavanger in Tromsø
discuss literature with ministers
and librarians
who we go to bed with
in hotel rooms and party. We party at festivals
in Molde in Odda at Lillehammer

and in all our country's small towns and in other countries
we fly from city to city
drink eat
and read for a few minutes to a public
we love and loath
and who we have sex with
at late-night parties in hotel rooms in student bedsits
in Harstad in Kristiansand in Fredrikstad
and everywhere
there's a literature house
or a library or at least a cafe
with an audience of seventeen
which keeps us
and our dreams
of immortality alive.

We autograph copies give lectures
get interviewed in the papers talk
nonsense about politics and literature
about our lives
as poor writers
in the rich oil nation of Norway
pumping out oil
which keeps us alive
and the so-called art we create
in our spare time
on those rare occasions when we're at home
away from the festivals
which take place everywhere

at all times
of the year.

We travel around like vagrants beggars
eating drinking
like the wealthy like aristocrats
we are the new aristocrats
we are the new proletariat
we are the new rebels
we are the new heroes
we are the new idiots
we are the new beggars
we are the new poor
we are the new dreamers
we are the new politicians
we are the new jesters
on Facebook in the papers on radio
and television in the periodicals and
the advertising campaigns
for ourselves.
We're the ones who tell the truth
about the state of the nation and its future
about the refugees and the wars
about climate crises and power politics
about feminism and threatened species
flood disasters Middle East oil drilling
Muslims capitalism religion
about philosophy art and literature
we're the ones
we are the new writers.

On Wednesday the eighth of October I receive a handsome
envelope in the mail
one of those exclusive envelopes
which remind me of letters from Janne
she always sent such lovely envelopes
even though what was in them could be dire
brown green red yellow envelopes
which I've gathered into a bundle
held together by two crossed elastic bands
it looks like a little packet
a letter packet
and this collection of letters
is my dearest possession.
The pale-yellow envelope
which arrived in the post today
its thick paper watermarked with
two letters
an H with an M superimposed like the loving embrace
of two characters
it's a royal watermark
and the letter is an invitation to dinner
at Skaugum.
I sit a long while in the living room
and imagine
this dinner at Skaugum.
Then I get out one of my best sheets of writing paper
and as politely as I can
pen my apologies.

He's a man who receives letters
many letters
long letters
he rarely answers them
doesn't read them either
only a few
from the same person
they're the letters
that destroy him utterly.
Some letters
contain dried flowers
nails pubic hair
bits of skin
spots of blood lipstick
touches
that don't touch him.

The most beautiful letter
he's ever received
was a metre wide
and one and a half metres long
a rolled-up canvas
of hand-painted hearts
some hearts red some hearts empty
forming a long script
of hearts line after line
the lines broken
by spaces white fields
unreadable as white writing

between the hearts.
It must have taken many weeks
perhaps months
to create the letter.
He had the letter framed in glass
hung the picture in the living room
at a distance from his writing table
now he could read it.
He read the letter over and over again
moving closer and further away
discovered different distances
and read the letter.
One day in September he took the train
to Oslo to meet the artist
who'd written the letter.
She arrived at their appointed
rendezvous in a taxi
and he sat in the back seat with her
they drove to his hotel
and made love.

One day a letter arrived
from New York
and this letter he answered.
He cycled into town
went into an ironmonger's
and had a copy of his house-key made.
He put the key into a padded envelope

and sent his letter without words
to the address in New York.

Some letters he reads
over and over again
it's peculiarly painful
to read
the letters she wrote
when she loved him.
I have never and will never
love anyone like I love you
he reads
over and over gain
as if the letters have the power
to conjure up
her love
many years after
she stopped loving him.

On Thursday the ninth of October I watch an Almodóvar film
in the basement room
Talk to Her.
Marco begins to cry because he's thinking
of a girlfriend he had ten years earlier.
It's the new girlfriend
he's got
ten years later
who causes the tears over his ex
the new love rekindles the old

and Marco cries again and again I've
never seen a man cry
so much in a film
it's ten years since he was dumped
and now Marco cries
and I cry with him
again and again.
Almodóvar knows a whole lot
about love.

Ten years I'm
halfway there.
Sophie Calle once said to me
when I was interviewing her at a literary festival
in Stavanger:
I only make love to men I don't like.
It sounded flippant
but I knew quite well what she meant
maybe she'd had a love affair
she didn't want to reawaken a regret
she didn't want to disturb
and when she made love to men
she didn't like
she avoided being reminded of
how painful it is to love.
Is that the answer
only to make love to someone you don't like
or should you keep to yourself?
That's the question

when you can't love.
And how long will you be alone
and how long can you be alone
can you live celibate
for the rest of your life?

During a dinner at Cecilie Løveid's
I announced suddenly
that I'd made up my mind
to be celibate.
There were two men and three women
around the table and the three women
all began to laugh
it was clear that the idea of a man
living without sex
was ludicrous and
Agathe Simon who was on a visit from Paris
tapped me on the shoulder and asked
if I wanted to join her on the steps
for a smoke. On the steps she said
what a good chat-up line that was
and then she laughed.
But I'm serious I said.
I've decided to live
without sex.
Have you lost the urge she asked
giving my arm a nudge. I noticed
her breasts beneath the man's
white shirt her short dark hair

and her eyes behind the thick glasses. No
I haven't lost the urge
it's a resolution I said.
I've a genuine desire to experience something new.
What new experience d'you think you'll have?
Well I don't know perhaps a greater
sensuality a more powerful feeling of presence
a deeper kind of love I think
towards the world and
towards things I said.

How long is this celibacy of yours going to last
Agathe Simon asked on the steps
where we were smoking.
I almost replied
until tonight Agathe
but I managed to contain the outburst
and I managed to arrive home alone
I left the dinner party drunk
and with a feeling that I'd passed
the first serious test and I
listened to the wind sighing in the trees
to the water trickling over the stones
in the river I glanced at the stars
shining in the night sky
and for the first time
I noticed
the juniper bush
that grew next to
my front door.

Friday the tenth of October and the birch tree in the garden
stands there alone
just outside the kitchen window.
For a long time I've never seen
this tree
perhaps because it's so close
so near the house and the front door
where I go in and out
alone
each and every day.

I've overlooked the birch tree
just as one ceases to greet the neighbour
a widower now
for fear he'll mention
his wife.

Now I see the birch tree.
Every morning when I'm having breakfast
and every evening
before I go to bed
the tree stands clearly detached
from the plum tree the blackcurrant bushes
and the rose tree with its white
flowers.
In the evening the trees huddle
closer together
in the darkness and become one large
dusky family.

And through the leaves in the light
from the window behind the birch tree
the flat where my neighbour lived
with his wife
is now occupied by a student
a young girl
who moves about the living room half-naked
whereas the old woman went from
table to table always dressed
always adorned for her husband
and for me.

How quickly time passes in a kitchen
it's only a few months since
the old lady was standing at the window
watering her flowers
with hair pinned up and mother-of-pearl earrings
dressed in a deep-yellow serge dress I
could almost smell
the last century through the chink
in the window and now the young
girl is walking about the same living room with
nothing but a G-string
between her buttocks
and a crop top
which sits like snow
just covering her breasts
and after only a few days
with this new neighbour

I've forgotten the old
world
completely.

Saturday the eleventh of October just yesterday a friend
collapsed while grouse shooting in the mountains
lay there in the heather with severe
palpitations. It was as if my heart wanted
to beat its way out of my body he told me on the phone
from the hospital where they were keeping him
a few days with wires attached to his chest
motionless at last.
This is the life
he said from his hospital bed. I'm being
really well-looked-after here.

And later on the phone: This is the best
thing that's happened to me. Dying
can't be all that bad
but the best thing
was surviving.

And later: I hope I can stay on
here for a few days and if you want to visit
me bring some red wine
in two Coke bottles.

Sunday the twelfth of October I cycle
to Haukeland University Hospital
walk with my head down

into the corridors take off my hat
keep my sunglasses on ever-afraid to see
disease to see death people are here to get well
but I see nothing but death
in pale-blue pyjamas coughing and limping
through the corridors. My paternal grandmother died here
grandfather
maternal grandparents my mother died here
soon it'll be my turn I always think
in the corridors of the hospital and follow
the designated red stripe on the floor
find K's room
on the second floor a light-green room
with six beds
he's been given the bed by the window
from where he's lying he has a view of the graveyard
outside.
He's propped up reading wires fixed to his chest
and his arm like a puppet's
with his long dark hair
across the white pillow
pale skin light pyjamas bits of plaster and tape
as when you glue an old doll together
he looks uncommonly well smiles
You've only got to pull that cord
he says. Then she'll bring us two glasses
you've brought the Coke along?
We open the bottles drink
the way we usually do.

I got what I deserved he says. We
shot too many grouse
the grouse have lost their colour you know
they were standing out white below the snow
and I shot the mother and daughters and the whole brood
I shot the last of the family
on the wing the shot hit her in the breast she
stuck out her wings and sailed through the air dead
down the mountainside over the treetops
she whizzed into the forest and disappeared he says.
I ran hell for leather down the mountain
and into the forest
ran round and round searching the bushes and undergrowth
beneath trees and rocks in the stream and the bog
in the heather in the grass in the moss but I couldn't
find her.
It began to get dark I
turned on my head torch tried
to pick her out
walked in the light from the beam now it would be difficult
to find my way back to my brother he'd
be waiting as agreed down by the car but
I had to find her and I couldn't find her.
Then I began to scramble over quickly
the way I'd run down and now
I felt my heart it was beating faster
than usual I stopped but my heart continued
at the same tempo it ran wild and then I fell
and lost consciousness for a moment opened my eyes now

I'm dying I thought there was nothing
to be done I said goodbye goodbye I said
and thanks for everything I said out loud
to the pines to the birches
farewell night sky farewell stars
farewell or hello here I come
Mum and Dad I thought and lay there
quite peacefully it was just a matter of surrendering
I surrendered it was the end
and perhaps because I'd surrendered
my heart slowed down now it's going to stop
now it has stopped now I'm dead
I thought and my thoughts were still there
so maybe only half of me is dead
so odd to be dead and alive
perhaps that's what death is like perhaps
we take our thoughts with us into death
I thought now the light will appear but the light
didn't appear it was just my head torch lighting
up the trees which pointed the way upward
but my heart continued to beat
I could feel it now I'm alive
luckily but then my mobile rang
it annoyed me here I am dying
and my mobile rings
it must be my brother I
found the phone in my jacket pocket well what
can I say I'm dying no I'm alive

I'm lying in the heather and I'm alive.
Get up carefully he said
it was like talking to God
on the phone. Get up carefully
and walk slowly down the mountain down
towards the car slowly he repeated
don't hang up maintain contact
while you walk my brother said.

Monday the thirteenth of October I wake up early
go out to the bathroom put
sticking plasters on my face
over my left eye over my nose
a plaster on my forehead a plaster on the corner of my
mouth
plaster over old scars and skin
that's been kissed
away with my eye away with my mouth
away with my nose
wrap a bandage round my chest
round and round round my chest
bandage round my chest secure
the end with a safety pin
and go back to bed.

It's Tuesday the fourteenth of October the day
begins with a gentle autumnal light subdued
by curtains and rain.
How nice to lie in bed

when the light's pressing against the window
and filling the bedroom with the usual
things bedside table a lamp books
a water glass the bedroom door
always open
and beyond the door three more doors
all leading to dark rooms.
They're filled with light a light
that settles on my daughter's bed
and objects in my daughter's room
on my girlfriend's clothes and things
in the deserted girlfriend room
the light steals through the house
like an unfamiliar animal
stirring up dust waking up the clothes
and the sleeping smells
now it smells faintly of material and boots
and past movement.
The first sound of water is it
the tap dripping in the bathroom
is it the rain is it the rain
in the dream is it the dream
in the rain are you asleep
are you dreaming are they both back
in their beds your girls
they aren't your girls
whose are they
your girls
where are they sleeping

my girls
they're not sleeping here
in their beds.

The day ends as it began
in bed the light that came goes
past the bedroom window.
How lovely to lie
beneath the curtains and watch
the day go by.
How lovely to lie
in bed
as the light is sucked out of the room
and takes the objects away with it
on a leash
there goes the bedside table
the lamp the books and the door with the light
that draws the bedroom with it
into the dream
of another place.

Wednesday the fifteenth of October.   The house
the same house a garden flowers   roses
but also vegetables herbs   fruit bushes   an apple tree.
Part of the garden grows wild weeds   and wild flowers
snowdrops in March crocus   daffodils   and later
white anemones then cress.   A well-trodden
path from the garden to the river   always poplars
in the spring willow and ash   birch in spring.
In the autumn oak and elm.

A copper beech red in autumn   chestnuts in autumn.
A hazel and perhaps in the morning   a squirrel.
In the evening a woodpecker   in the evening two owls.
At night dogs   at night
you don't know what's prowling   round   the house.
At night a light in the window on the first floor   in the room
over   the river   a bed
or bunk blankets bookshelves
but also books on the floor on the writing table.   A chair
flowers in vases a water glass two pens   a knife.
And now   as then
a figure in the room sitting hunch-backed
round-shouldered bent from many years of writing.

Francesco Petrarca wrote:
As I approached my fortieth year although still filled
with the strength and ardour of youth I turned my back so entirely
upon my urges that I even expunged the memory of them
and it was as if I'd never even seen a woman.

Of my anguished life, its many torments.

So wrong are the paths of lust.

I ask my sigh to call you by name.

I turn at every step I take.

A bitter rain of tears blinds me.
The young woman by the green laurel.

When the tree shifts from the soil it grows in.

How weak is the thread that holds.

The closer I am to the last days.

If only I believed that death could liberate me.

I loved and I love these places.

I shall hate this window for ever.

She came so often and comforted me in dreams.

I see no straw to clutch at anywhere.

My face betrays what my heart feels.

Could flame perhaps be doused by a flame.

I stand and listen; I learn nothing new.

To wish for night and hate the red of dawn.

In the mirror I often see the sentence passed.

Oh day, oh hour, the final moment.

A life of haste never ceases in its flight.

It's only wind, only shade, this goodness.

You let us stand sunless in the cold of darkness.

There came a time for peace, now, truce.
Blessed be day and month, the year.

On a day in October
six young men
we don't know how old they are
fifteen sixteen seventeen eighteen
we'll be able to tell that they're young
they won't be wearing masks

they'll want to show us their faces
their skin colour
their discontent
they'll want to show us a ruined future
they'll want to show us their youth
which they'll blow to bits.

On a day in October
we don't know when or where
six young men will
dress themselves in explosives
comb their hair tie their shoelaces
put on their best shirts
and go into the city.
It's Friday or Saturday
the city's lights shine
from the cafes the clubs the restaurants the windows
where everyone can see out
but not everyone can come in.

We see these loving couples who eat
these rich young people who drink
these successful city-types who party
who carouse who dance who discuss
the war
in other lands
at the restaurant tables in these bright spots
that will turn dark
these six young comrades
will go in there

for the first and last time.
Perhaps the six boys are called
Bilal Amine Samy Salah Abdelhamid Ibrahim
such lovely names
which will be destroyed
which will destroy
other names
as lovely
just as all names are lovely
before they're destroyed.

On a day in October
six young men
will bring the war back to their cities
and the war that had been foreign
in unseen cities
will become visible
where the strangers live
in our cities.
The war will be waged by young men
against restaurant-goers loving couples friends
and girlfriends who have no inkling they're to die
one Friday evening
in town.

What kind of war is it
that isn't even called a war?
A war without name
it's called faith and god
its called love and death

it's called eternity and now
it has all the beautiful words
on its side
that nameless war
called us and them
called Samy and Salah
called Charlotte and Anna
called Friday and Saturday
called October November
which has all the beautiful names
on its side
this war against the present
day and the coming
day
this war against the days and the months
and the year
it has no name
it's called nothing.
And how can we fight against
something that has no name
that contains all names and words
within its nameless complexity?

We say terror and violence
we could say destruction
we could say I'm destroying you now
my brother my mother my child
my love my father my house my street
my life I'm destroying everything now

we could say
but we don't know the correct word
for our crimes
we don't know the true word
for the war we're waging
against ourselves
and our dearest.
We say climate change and catastrophe
we could say floods and deluges
forest fires and drought
poverty and starvation
famine and war
which we wage on others
but we don't say it
because we don't know the name
of the war we fight
we don't know the word
for our daily devastations.
We could say I'm driving a car in the city
I'm flying from Oslo to Gran Canaria
I'm on the boat between Bergen and Hirtshals
I'm eating my steak and drinking my wine
I'm shopping at the Duty Free
I'm buying Gucci and Louis Vuitton
I'm walking through the streets of Paris
or London
I'm meeting my girlfriend
in New York.
We could say I am innocent

for as yet we don't know the name
of that offence
that is ignorance
of the consequences of our amusements
and our freedom.

Kamilla phones and asks
if I want to come to Oslo
visit her in Oslo
but the only thing I want to do in Oslo
is to beat up a man
punch in his left eye break his nose
smash his mouth kick him in the chest
break his ribs and have him sent away
to hospital
so that he'll be able to understand
how I'm feeling
what damage a friend
can do to a friend
that's what I think about
when I think of Oslo.
And so I'M NOT GOING TO OSLO
I'm straining every sinew
to keep myself at home I
can't visit Kamilla
don't want to visit friends
can't go to events in Oslo
for fear of what
I might start doing

to my friend
if I meet him in Oslo
and so I won't go to Oslo
and the fact that I won't go to Oslo
is solely down to my love
for his girlfriend.

Saturday the first of November and I'm
going to take the train to Oslo.
Awoken early by a dream it's
four- five- six o'clock and I'm wide
awake what was it who was it
who woke me a face a voice
a sentence that keeps me awake
that gets me out of bed into the bathroom
on with my clothes
on with my makeup
my mother's wig.
Pack my bag
button my coat lace my boots
down the steps out of the door
sprint to the end of the gravel path
on to the bus to the morning train.

Killer
don't think
act.

At last
I'm the person I want to be

the person I was
once before
if I remember rightly.

Killer-boy
if anyone injured you
you hurt them
back.

As simple as that.

So right so pure.

You fought
it was what you knew
what you did
if anyone challenged
or crossed your territory
if any
boys or men
did you harm.

You've got a broken heart
you confide in a friend
and this friend listens.
What you say arouses an interest
in him a desire he wants what you had
perhaps he falls in love
but even so
he should have kept away
because now he turns what was good

into something bad
he wrecks a friendship
and he wrecks your relationship
with the girl you were with.
So what are you going to do about it?
Aren't you going to do anything?
Are you going to let it go?
Are you going to be nice and understanding?
Are you going to lie there in bed consumed
with anguish and fury?
Are you going to lie there and feel the lash
of these words: despair and betrayal?
Are you going to lie there with images of him
who waits for her
who holds her hand
who undresses her and
makes love to her
on the bed you lay in?
How long can you lie there like that?
Sleepless. Sick. Destroyed by jealousy and hate.
November November.
I buy some newspapers
a bottle of water
find my seat by the window
look out
watch the pigeons fly up
the houses starting to move
the trees walking
the sun rises the city wakes

and vanishes.
At last
I'm doing what I should making
a move
in the wrong direction.

I've always liked travelling
by train
the Bergen–Oslo
route especially
but in the opposite direction
it's always better going home
than setting out.
I don't want to visit Oslo
but I'm not going unwillingly I
travel out of necessity
like a business trip
one would rather avoid
but which has to be made
to straighten the accounts.
I'm travelling as a woman.
I don't know why.
Perhaps because it's my mother's birthday
she'd have been eighty today
Saturday the first of November
and we've hardly got to Voss
before I'm ordering a half-bottle of red wine
in the restaurant car.
I speak with my mother's voice

it's the voice of the dead
a necessary voice
for what I shall do in Oslo.
The dead shall talk to the dead.
My friend is already dead
but I want to speak to him
as if he's still alive.
It will cause pain.
It will hurt to be
humiliated by a woman.
I could have injured him as a friend
but I'd rather damage him as someone else.
I don't know him any more.
I want to speak to him like a mother.
With a light voice lighter than normal.
November is the right month.
Janne and I are Scorpios.
We have this in common.
This venom.
That must be expressed.
I read the newspaper.
Violence.
War.
Accidents.
Floods.
Earthquakes.
Catastrophes.
Many dead.
Injured.

Good.

I order a half-bottle of white wine.

Look out through the train window.

White trees.

Frozen water.

The first snow.

A simple breakfast meal.

Coffee.

A cigarette on the platform.

Finse.

Frost.

A winter's journey.

In autumn.

November November.

The train's rhythm.

Soporific.

Are you asleep?

Can you tell that I'm on my way?

An animal.

Look for an animal in your dreams.

A dog attacks a dog.

It's natural.

Such and such.

Such and such and such and such.

Closer now.

Such and such and such and such and such.

Soporific.

Are you awake?

It's morning.
In a few hours it'll be dark.

I awake to the tinny voice
saying Oslo Central
and feel a reluctance to leave the train
fix my eyes on a random neck and
follow the stranger using his movements out
off the train towards the station concourse
where I get in the queue
for the ticket windows
buy a return ticket on the night train
in the sleeping car I'll
try to sleep
on the journey home.
How lovely it will be to travel home
in hardly more than seven hours' time
a short day's work
that's all
then I can rest content
that I've done what
had to be done.
Such and such.
I go out into the city.
Must do some good things
before I do what isn't good.
To walk up the main street watch
the crowd feel a stranger
that's always good.

Walk in a throng
on Karl Johansgate buy a pair of sunglasses
walk facing the sun with the sun in my eyes
piercing.

Everything that's painful
can be nice
walking in places where you walked together
visiting the painful places the romantic places
a bookshop a certain cafe
and the park surrounding the palace where you always
walked as a couple
hand-in-hand in summer and spring
and once in the autumn
in November
to celebrate her birthday
in the Kunstnernes Hus restaurant where
the waiter always greeted the pair of you as if you
were old acquaintances a well-known couple
one of the couples who'd be together
for ever
back then
before it ended.

Now I walk alone through the park
just to gather sufficient
strength and rage and sorrow
to be able to do the thing
I'm going to do.
He works in a bookshop.

I'll stand outside the shop
and wait for him.
Follow him a little way
perhaps he'll walk towards the flat
where she lives
perhaps he'll take the route
I used to use.
I know just where I'll strike
there's a small lacuna a no-man's-land
on the rise near Henrik Wergeland's house just before
the Thon Hotel a little space
just big enough for me
and him.
Sometimes we'd kiss
in that very spot
like a little rest
a breather on the hill
just there.
I've got plenty of time
it's still several hours before the bookshop
closes I'll walk up Bogstadveien like I
used to visit the second-hand bookshop where I'd
look for the book I could never get hold of
perhaps I'll find it today
perhaps today is a good day
perhaps I'll eat at a restaurant
perhaps I'll have a bottle of wine
perhaps I'll be drunk
when I meet him

that cur
that piece of scum
who is her lover.

I walk up Bogstadveien
my favourite street in Oslo
I don't know why perhaps
because the street rises
rises out of city out of the centre
and its ascent
like all ascents holds
a promise of something different
something loftier and better
above the city
on the heights
a new city
with fresher air
and thinner people
who cycle and walk
and live in simple houses
in a communist society
closer to nature
without cars and over-consumption
of goods and electricity and money
but it isn't like that
not on Bogstadveien and not
on other eminences above other cities
quite the opposite
the higher above the city you go

the bigger the cars and houses
the higher above the city you go
the further away communism and
the dream of a bright future seems
it's as if you're sinking as you walk upward
deeper and deeper
into malevolence and inanity
and by the time you reach Majorstuen
and the intersection there
your only desire
is to walk back down Bogstadveien
towards the city centre.
I walk down Bogstadveien
find a restaurant where you can eat outside
with patio heaters you can be warm
in the cold smoke and eat
and drink a bottle of wine
which is essential
for the intoxication
that impairs the judgement
and instils the madness
necessary to knock a man down.
It's been a long time since I fought since
I found any pleasure in it
for many years I trained myself to keep away from
disorder and trouble
melt away as they say
not to argue not to get worked up about anything
at all at one time I managed

to turn it into a kind of sport people
could say anything to me
and I wouldn't react
often someone would come up to me
in bars at venues
and try their hardest to provoke me
I thoroughly enjoyed it
sat there calmly listening
taking all their curses and swearing
which in a way I approved
they'd once been my own.
But I'd laid them aside
just as I'd shed
the extraneous movements
of hands and feet
I practised sitting still
and listening
I became good at being on the receiving end
and keeping quiet.
But never before has anyone done me such hurt
as this friend I confided in
he knew well knew so well how incredibly
fond I was of Janne and that our rift
was literally killing me
and yet he chose
to start a relationship with her I
still don't know how he dared to
it needs a certain courage a certain strength
and perhaps a devilry and

spite or madness
which at any rate more than qualifies him
to face me I think
in Bogstadveien and make ready to leave.
I pay the bill in cash.
Tighten my bootlaces.
Button my coat.
Swing my arms as I walk
jog
to get my circulation going
loosen up my shoulders arms
increase my heart rate
the heat of my body
a warm-up.
Breathe through my nose
clench my fists
small quick steps
jump
dance I
realize I'm drunk
suddenly get a fit of laughing
nervousness that's good I'll
land up in jail
but what I'll teach my friend
about friendship
is worth a few months in a cell
I think on Bogstadveien and pass
Lorry and the Literature House
pass the Artists' House and say farewell

to these places which once were mine
which once were ours
they seem alien now
as if they belong to a different life
my life with Janne
which will soon be over.

The time is ten to seven I
find a place to wait
a little way from the bookshop
with a good view of the street
illuminated by street lights and the last of the daylight
a blue duskiness veils the pedestrians
and robs them of their faces
if only it would begin to snow
everything would be perfect
for something red I
light a cigarette
almost happy
at how beautiful everything is
when you hate.

In a few minutes the bookshop will close
the lights in the shop will go out and everything
will happen just as I've imagined it
so many times.
He'll come out on to the pavement
a tall thin figure dark-haired
unshaven an arty type I
can see that he's beautiful that was why

I liked him his fine looks
his sensitivity his loneliness
he always walks alone
perhaps he'll light a cigarette
before he sets off
but now I see something I hadn't anticipated
a figure emerges from the street on the left
which causes my heart to beat faster it's
Janne I recognize the hat and coat
and the way she walks I almost call out
to her shout
a warning
but I manage to stifle it
as she walks up to meet him and embrace him
just as she used to walk up to me
and embrace me.
Suddenly it's as if I'm seeing
myself being hugged
and in that instant I feel a sympathy
for him
and for the person I was
when I was loved.
Is it her love for him
or for me that holds me back?
I turn away
look for somewhere I can conceal myself
better I mustn't can't destroy
her love
for me

I can't mustn't destroy
her love
for him.
I can't destroy the love
that's hers.
I walk quickly away
from what I'd imagined and planned
bend over behind a bush
vomit and get a
nosebleed it's as if all the punches
I haven't managed to land gather themselves up
and let loose on my own body hammer away
at my stomach and kidneys
at my nose and eyes
everything turns black and I
collapse.

In the station precincts there's a restaurant
Egon also has outside tables
with patio heaters I'm cold
wipe away congealed blood
with a napkin
rinse my mouth with water
drink bad wine eat
mediocre pizza and watch the stream
of people setting out or returning from
a journey.
It's a quarter past ten on Saturday evening
the first of November and I'm drunk
and proud of what I haven't done

in Oslo.
How lovely it is to drink.
How lovely it is to eat at a tacky
restaurant and maybe
it's at just such a place as this
that one can make an important decision.
I dig out a pen and notebook
jot down this one sentence
as if it's a law
a commandment
which mustn't be forgotten.
Then I stagger off towards the station
towards the platforms and this one railway line
out of the city and over the mountains at night.
It may be that on such a night
in a berth on the sleeper crossing the mountains
you'll forget all that's difficult
in the world you lie beneath clean white sheets
in a bunk that rocks through the night
and perhaps
before you fall asleep
you'll sense a deep dark joy
about all the things you won't do.

~

November, November.

I'd like to die
before my father I

don't want to watch
him die.

There's a limit
to how much death
one can tolerate.

My mother's death.
Agnete's death I
bore that.

I didn't get ill.
I didn't fall apart.

And the break with Janne
I bore that too.

Losing someone
who hasn't died
is almost worse
than losing a person
who's gone
for good.

Living with a loss of love
and the person you love
loves someone else.

It's a song.

A November song.

A love song
in November.

I love you.
It won't end.

The song doesn't end either.
There are others too who'll sing it.

The Petrarch song.
The pop song.

The song about the only one.
It's a song that'll last for ever.

It's a song that will be sung
after the singer is gone.

Great love exists
the sort that can kill you.

And if you survive this love
you'll live like someone half-dead
you'll live half a life.

There's a relationship in the half-life
which is real
the relationship with death.

You're not frightened of dying
sometimes you want it
that's natural

it's not something to hush up
or be ashamed of
there's a huge heavy force
in the wish to die
in the yearning to vanish
which increases with the years
day by day
that's natural
you're drawn towards death
with the same force
that once drew you
towards life
and perhaps a good death
is the one that's slow
that takes a long time
a slow suicide
that really lets you get acquainted with
death
in all death's stages
a slow descent
into a world which gradually
grows darker
or lighter
and which vanishes
or comes into view
what do you know about dying
before you make up your mind to it
or before death enters
your life like an inevitability

you can choose
or be chosen
and in both cases there's an opportunity
not to flee
not to renounce death
but to receive what is to come
the unknown
with the same awareness
the same concentration
the same curiosity
with which you greeted life yes
you'll die with a fifteen-year-old's
desire and determination
and you'll think of death
as something new
as something good
as a lover
as the ultimate orgasm
you'll have
with that dark woman
which is your final relationship yes
you think of death as a woman
and no one in the world can rob you of
this notion
this love
which is your last.

When you prepare yourself for death
it may be possible to

die well
even though death will be painful
and unpleasant I recall now
that I read how Rilke
didn't want any painkillers
or other drugs on his death bed
he wanted to be conscious when he died.
And I remember the depiction of old
Chamberlain Brigge's death
in *The Notebook of Malte Laurids Brigge*
where Rilke allows the old man to die
a slow and terrible death.
And what a death: two long months
and his screams so loud that they could be heard
as far as the tenants' farm.
The old man dies a death which suits him
and which all through life he'd harboured within him
and nourished
Rilke writes
and how would Chamberlain Brigge
have reacted if someone had demanded
he die a different death
from the one
Rilke writes.
He lets the old man die his own death
just as he died his own death himself
just as we shall all die our own deaths
even when we try to run away from them
or allow death to be anaesthetized

with expectations and lies
with drugs and reassurances
hidden and shut away in a booth of death
alone in a sickroom.

When Agnete died
she was the mother of my daughter
and her sister
she wanted to die at home.
She lay in the bedroom
with her two girls
playing around her
while she died.
The girls climbed into her bed
and slept with her
while she was dying.
It was a death
that filled the entire house
and us we who lived there
for many months
it was a death
that marked us through all the years
we lived in the house
and which still lives in us
even now we've moved on to other houses
and other lives which carry this death
within them as long as we're alive.
Agnete's death
will always live

in us who experienced it
so intimate and tangible day and night
with all of death's smells and sounds
with death's silence
and the sudden outbursts
of fear and anger
of anguish and incomprehensible words
which came from an alien place
a place we recognized
as the place of death it
had moved into
our life.
We received death
like an unwanted gift.
We didn't know it then
but death would open
our lives one morning we noticed
the rain as something new we
could no longer distinguish the rain
from our joys from the dark
mornings of autumn
and when the wind blew it blew
through us
and when the leaves fell from the trees
we sat silently by the kitchen window
it was no longer possible to keep
nature separate from our days and nights
in the house on Askøy
where the grass grew unchecked in the garden

and the roses shed their blossoms with a heaviness
and beauty we hadn't seen before.
One evening we discovered that there were
bats hanging from a beam in the attic
and the bees hummed outside the bedroom window
where the rhododendron bushes pushed their twigs
through the cracked pane
rats and mice sought refuge
in walls and gaps
flies found their crannies
where they could die and overwinter
and between the kitchen floorboards
spiders and beetles crept
cobwebs were woven in the window frames
and ants made a thin black line
across the kitchen surface it was just before
the first snow came and filled the house
with a new white light sometimes
we heard doors open and close
the stairs creaked the cold arrived
and it was as if the deceased
was also searching for a place to overwinter
in the house.

November came.

Our winter in a month.

It's the twelfth of November my birthday
and my father's coming to dinner

from the kitchen window I watch his car arrive
and decide not to chide
him for driving and not walking as we've
agreed he's almost given up walking
and I must stop struggling against death
if he wants to lose his legs and mobility
I'll have to let him get on with
it even though it annoys me
that now I can't give him any wine with
his meal I'll have to drink the wine myself
when he's driven back home I'll
have to celebrate this birthday alone
once he's eaten and taken himself home.
He comes through the door with a laboured
slowness that hurts me but I
embrace him and welcome him
dinner's ready I say
and he holds out a plastic bag with
something he's bought inside a present
for the first time in my life
I get a bottle of wine from my father.
Now we've got something to drink with the meal he says.
But you can't have wine if you're
driving I say.
He snorts
does it matter if I have
a glass or two of wine it's your
birthday
many happy returns he says.

I open the bottle and fill the glasses
we have halibut and mashed potato drink
the wine toast
congratulations on reaching fifty-two he says.
I'm fifty-four I say.
How time flies
faster and faster with each passing year
it doesn't seem that long since we celebrated
your fortieth birthday you were with
Monica then he says.
I was with Agnete then I say.
Yes of course he says
how are things with Janne I miss her
couldn't you ask her to visit us she
moved out so quickly I wasn't able to say
goodbye properly he says.
She's written a book I say.
A book her as well what's it about he asks.
It's about love I say.
Have you read it he asks.
No it's coming out in April.
In April he says
that was the month I met your mother.
And now he starts crying.
And she died in April he says.
But let's talk about something pleasant
it's your birthday have you
found another girlfriend he asks.
No I say.

You're far too young and eligible
to be on your own.
I'm beginning to show my age I say.
Fifty-one is nothing
when I was your age
and then he begins to cry again.
When you were my age I was
twenty-six I say pouring wine
into the glasses.
Ah twenty-six he says tell me d'you
miss your mother at all.
I don't miss people who're dead I say.
Well you're the hard sort he says
quite different from me.
Do you miss your mother I ask.
No I don't not really
it was such a long time ago he says.
It's seventeen years since my mother died I say.
Is it that long ago it
feels like yesterday.
That's because you loved her I say.
Have you got something stronger to go with the coffee he asks.
You drink too much I say.
You do too he says.
You try to hide it he says.
You do too I say.
I get out the other bottle of wine and
offer my father a cigarette.
Now you'll have to leave the car here I say.

Does it matter
how I die he says.
Perhaps not for you but for me
it does I'd like you to live
to a ripe old age I say.
And now I begin to cry.
You know perfectly well that I live for you
and your sister and for the grandchildren
if it had been up to me
I'd have been dead long since
I wanted to die when you mother died he says.
You should have found yourself a new partner I say.
It's not possible to find anyone new
when you're still in love he says.
But the one you love is dead I say.
And the one you love has left
it's the same thing he says.
And now we both begin to laugh.
I've inherited all your diseases
the crying the drinking the loving
unto death
I say and pour wine into the glasses.
And you and I both like to be alone
so give me a bottle of wine he says
I know you've got several bottles in the cupboard
under the sink well
that was my hiding place too
then I'll drive home and drink mine
and you drink yours and

so we'll each celebrate
your birthday
the way we like best
alone
with a bottle of wine and
all our dead he says.

The guests arrive one by one
some in pairs it's snowing
a delicate white carpet falling flake
by flake numberless snowflakes
falling in the dark small flakes of light
in the wind which blows the guests in
as if they're shadows flickering
in the dusk this way and that in the wind
until they find their way up the drive
along the gravel with its covering of snow
they follow each other's tracks
and enter frozen at the door
brushing snow from their coats
first Erling and Aagot
my mother's parents he's tall and thin
with walking stick and hat thick round glasses
which magnify the grey-blue eyes
and make his face milder than it is
a sharp face whose features have formed
themselves into an accusation or discontent
no one knows what it is that troubles him
he never complains she is small and dark

a shrivelled body distilled by bitterness
a woman with great expectations
which have never been fulfilled
it's given her figure a kink
in the middle it's impossible to tell if she's going
fall or take a step forward
the couple hang up their coats
and are shown into the living room
seat themselves in the chairs that once were their own
ah now they're in position and here come
Alfred and Elly Alice the lovely Elly
so like Janne so like herself when she
was twenty-six and still childless
she's taller than her husband
Alfred Johan who shelters behind her
who pushes her in front of him
even though everyone can see he's a handsome
little man with longish dark hair
which he's carefully combed over a shiny pate
brown warm eyes which Elly Alice my father's mother
always describes as kindly eyes he has kindly
eyes and adores his wife just as everyone adores
Elly Alice she's the adored one.
My mother arrives alone
delayed she likes being late
it's a demonstration of obstinacy
and loneliness she always turns up alone
hand in hand with this loneliness
an invisible partner we always have to cater

for as if he's her real husband
the husband she should have had
but who never existed
anywhere in the world.
Perhaps he's responsible for making her late
for making her sit too long before the mirror on her dressing table
and rejecting too many clothes
before she finally emerged from the bathroom I
greet her with compliments
as I usually do she possesses an ardent beauty
designed by Estée Lauder and a Spanish wig-maker
the silver jacket she wears is a Chanel copy
she's made herself she's made her own
loose black trousers now she seats herself
by her parents it's impossible to tell
that she's their daughter
just as it's impossible to see
that I'm her son.
How does a family coalesce?
A family is stitched together from unmatched patches
forced into a pattern
the pattern that's called a family.
One can imagine the materials
being torn into strips
and each strip wanting to stand out on its own
as a trouser leg or
a flag.
Now Agnete blows in
through the door accompanied by two strange men

and this is her particular hallmark or brand
to be surrounded by men
and without these men she'd almost
be invisible
her relationship to the men is
like the female figure to the unicorn in a
tapestry she'd have no story
but for these men
and so she replaces them
with new men
who all weave the same tale
the tale of the doomed woman
the one who's never alone
the one who'll never be loved.
You can shout right into her face I
love you but her ears aren't ears
her eyes aren't eyes and her face
isn't a face but a piece of painted protective padding
she's suspended between herself and the person who's shouting.
I say welcome and who are these two men
you've got with you and she gives a small shrug
a gesture she's copied from Stefania Sandrelli
or Sophia Loren.
I've laid the table exactly
as my mother would have
with a white damask tablecloth white
place mats with silver floral
embroidery white dinner plates silver cutlery
crystal glasses candlesticks wine carafes

all these inherited objects
that have accumulated in the house
where almost nothing is mine
the house is a repository for the effects and
furniture of the dead the dining table the coffee table
the lamps the chairs the bookcases the paintings
the photographs and the letters in their
cardboard boxes in the attic the departed's declarations of love
and memories everything is preserved here in this house
including jewellery and watches
a whole heap of clothing
hats and sticks
spectacles and coins
as well as my maternal grandfather's entire record collection
he was an opera-lover and during the course of the evening
selected arias will be played
but now we eat we sit around the long table
and consume a fish soup made from a stock
of halibut bones and prawn shells with
carrots and salmon pieces.
We drink a dry white German wine
my grandfather stands and raises his glass.
Many happy returns he says we
hope you'll soon be coming to visit us.
I'll look forward to that too I say
and drink a toast
with my family.

How to live alone

I smoke twenty cigarettes
a day
drink two bottles of wine
it's a good life
that will end in a good death
just as I want it
whether it's painful and drawn out
or sudden
as when you turn a light out
in the bathroom
you fall to the floor
in the shower or on the way out of the shower
or perhaps you're sitting up
in bed and die there
or perhaps you collapse on the street
in the middle of a crowd of people who walk past
and perhaps one of the passers-by
tries to resuscitate you
but it's impossible to help you
with this death it's your own
and so ordinary so commonplace
in every city
perhaps you're cycling very fast
through the city streets
and fall off the bike just as you're
taking a corner you
love corners
and topple off the bike on the corner
or maybe you're sitting alone

in a cafe and your head hits the table
like dropping a puppet on the floor
or perhaps you're lying in bed with
a book and a cigarette and a glass
of something strong and the whole thing catches fire
and turns into a funeral pyre
the way they burn corpses in India
or perhaps you die next to a friend
in bed or with a stranger at a discotheque
at night in the dark splintered
by disco lights I love
men and women
and the loveliest is always
the individual not the sex or skin colour
not the country of origin or culture
but the person
standing before you
dressed or naked I don't
like thinking that someone from Norway
is a better man or woman
than a man and woman from Sri Lanka
or that a person from Syria
is worse than a person from Germany
and I hope that one day we'll be forced
to see the beauty in a stranger
and that what we call native land
will be overrun with foreignness
making it a better land
a better home

for all strangers
you too are a stranger
the moment you travel
or receive a visit
perhaps you're a stranger
in your own family
and with friends
even to your lover
you are a stranger
and you don't know yourself.
I hope one day we'll be forced
to love animals and plants
as much
as we love human beings
and perhaps you'll die in the open
in the heart of a forest
under a pine tree
next to an anthill
or you stumble in the river slip
on a stone and fall
into the cold rushing water
where your heart stops.
To sink to the bottom of a tarn
or be carried by sea currents back
to the water you came from
maybe it'll be worse than that
you'll spend months lying
in bed wrestling with pain
and nightmares

a long appalling mortal combat
which sucks the life out of you
day after day
night after night.
I've seen it
the way you shrivel
the way your body is consumed
by pain and ulcers
a skin that cracks
arms that sleep
feet that rot
as if you're really nothing more
than a plant
that's losing its colour
and fading away.
A plant-body now
in so much pain with
so little light and water
so much darkness
that you want nothing more
than to die.
The good death.